HEIDI
GROWS UP

The
GOLDEN PRESS
Classics Library

by Charles Tritten

Johanna Spyri's Translator

Illustrated by June Goldsborough

GOLDEN PRESS
Western Publishing Company, Inc., Racine, Wisconsin

Library of Congress Catalog Card Number 66-10792

Contents

FOREWORD

IT MUST HAVE REQUIRED considerable courage upon the part of Charles Tritten to fulfill the promise of the last chapter of *Heidi,* one of the most dearly beloved of all children's books, and to bring to a happy close the adventures of the little girl who grew up in the hills of Dörfli. Even for one who had translated all of Johanna Spyri's tales into French and was as familiar with her people and her country as she had been, it must have required long contemplation before he took up at last the pleasant task of writing a sequel to *Heidi.*

And yet there were so many reasons why *Heidi Grows Up* should have been written. Millions of children, as well as millions of "such as love children" (to whom Frau Spyri's books were always dedicated), pleaded with her during her lifetime to tell them what became of the little Alpine girl and the Alm-Uncle and Peter and Clara and all the rest. When no sequel was forthcoming during those twenty-one years between *Heidi*'s publication and its author's death in Zurich in 1901, the public began to turn to the many translators who were making the Spyri books (already accepted as classics in Germany and Switzerland) available to the children of other lands far from the mountains and lakes and valleys where the author spent all of her life.

In time these stories, written from the inexhaustible well-spring of Frau Spyri's memories of her own childhood, for one reason or another went into public domain, and the character of Heidi, like David Copperfield and D'Artagnan and Ivanhoe and Alice and Hans Brinker and Jim Hawkins, became the property of new generations of children the world over.

So little is known of the life and career of Johanna Spyri that it is not generally known that *Heidi* actually was begun shortly after the year 1870 while Europe was being torn by the Franco-Prussian War. She was then forty-three years of age and had for eighteen years been the wife of Bernhard Spyri, county clerk of Zurich. The book was not published, however, until 1880. Many of the book's unforgettable scenes and characters are the fond recollections of her own childhood in the hamlet of Hirzel where she was born in the "doctor's" house in July, 1827. The white house on its little green hill which was her birthplace still stands a few miles outside the city of Zurich. From its upper windows one can look across the forests of dark firs and catch a glint of blue which is Lake Zurich. "Hanneli" was the fourth child of Doctor Johann Jacob Heusser and his wife Meta Schweizer. Johann Heusser was the village's leading physician and Meta enjoyed considerable local fame as a poet and song writer.

The village school to which Johanna was sent with her brothers and sisters originally had been an old barn in a turnip patch. Surely her teacher must have been a dull sort to mistake her shyness for inattentiveness and to humiliate her before all the rest as the class dunce. As a result she disliked formal schooling so intensely that her understanding father finally withdrew her and sent her to another school held in the home of the village pastor. Like Frau Spyri herself, Charles Tritten has drawn upon the author's own childhood in writing this story of Heidi's later years. Thus Heidi's school days and her days as teacher in the village of Dörfli, as developed in *Heidi Grows Up,* have much in common with Johanna Spyri's girlhood, also her love of music and her interest in the birds and flowers of the Alpine fields and forests near her home.

Like Johanna, too, Heidi grown-up had little curiosity for what lay beyond the mountain run of her home village. She came back from her school days at Hawthorn happy in the knowledge that she would spend all of her life among the beloved friends of her childhood. We know that Frau Spyri lived her whole life happily and contentedly within a few miles of Zurich. Four years after the publication of *Heidi* her dear husband and understanding companion passed away. Their only son had died in childhood some years before. Widowed at fifty-three, Frau Spyri lived on at Zurich quietly writing her many tales of the children of the hills who carve wooden toys or care for the village goats high up among the steep

Alpine summer pastures. And as these tales won wider and wider fame in the world outside, the author of *Heidi* shrank more and more from public acclaim. She sincerely wished to avoid having "her innermost, deepest soul laid bare to human eyes," a desire which authors as a rule are not too prone to emulate nowadays.

And so, after a rich and full and fruitful life, Johanna Spyri passed away within a few miles from her birthplace and within a few days of her seventy-fourth birthday just when the beautiful Alpine summer was warming the high slopes of her beloved valley.

Was it prophetic, perhaps, that the last chapter of *Heidi* should have been entitled "Promises to Meet Again"? Now, years afterward, when the first enraptured readers of the first book have grandchildren of their own, the curtain is rolled back and we *do* meet again the little girl we left so long ago in the hut on the mountainside together with all her friends, and remain close to them while Heidi grows to lovely womanhood fulfilling all the sweet promises of her early years.

The children of today, and their parents as well, owe a debt of gratitude to Charles Tritten, not merely because he has rolled back that curtain and fulfilled the promise of the last chapter, but for the way in which he has done it, for the way he has made us feel once again the warm sun and the smell of the spring flowers high up on the mountain meadows, for his simplicity and understanding of young children embarked upon the breathless adventure of growing up.

10

The School at Rosiaz

1

AT NINE O'CLOCK one evening a very shy-appearing little girl stepped off the train at the big station in Lausanne. She stood for a moment looking about her in bewilderment, a blanket roll and suitcase at her feet, her precious violin case hugged tightly under her arm. Her name was Heidi and she had come all the way from Dörfli, a little mountain village high up in the Alps. Her grandfather and the good doctor who shared their winter quarters in the village wished her to finish her education in a cultured school. But it was not without great sacrifice that she had been sent to the fashionable boarding school from which her friend, Clara, had just graduated. Clara had traveled with her, and now, while the big train still stood snorting and whistling in the station, she leaned from the window and smiled. Clara knew all about the school, and Heidi wished very much that her friend could continue the journey with her and stay on another term. Perhaps the older girl guessed this, for she was doing her best to be cheerful, speaking very loud to make her voice heard above the noise of the puffing engine.

"It's going to be lots of fun, you'll see!" she cried gaily. "Dancing lessons and everything. I wonder if you'll have polite Monsieur Lenoir, who is always so smart-looking. 'Lightly, young ladies, and with grace,' he always used to tell us. 'Lightly and with grace,'" she repeated. "Heidi, you can imagine how wonderful it was for me to dance lightly and with grace. But you don't need to be taught that," she added. "You have always danced."

"I have not always played the violin," Heidi answered.

"You will love Monsieur Rochat," Clara continued with enthusiasm. "He is like the doctor in many ways. And in many other ways he is much like the grandfather. He has the same bushy brows."

Heidi gave a little jump of delight, seeing him already in her mind.

"Mademoiselle Raymond is very nice, too," Clara continued. "They are all nice in the school, though some may seem stern until you get to know them. Now don't forget to remember me to Mademoiselle Larbey!"

She caught sight of a tall and very English-looking

woman who was hurrying toward them along the platform.

"Ah, Miss Smith," she called as the teacher came up. "Good evening. How are you? Here is my friend, Heidi. She feels a little strange, you know, just at first. She has come all the way from Dörfli, just up from Maienfeld. But the train is starting again!" she cried as it gave her a warning jolt. "Good-bye, Heidi! Write to me soon. Good-bye! Good-bye!"

Miss Smith waved her gloved hand until the train was out of sight. But Heidi didn't move. She only hugged her violin more tightly to her side, feeling quite deserted now that Clara, her last link with home, had disappeared.

The Englishwoman turned to her.

"So you are the new student, Clara's friend. She often spoke of you and your grandfather as well as Peter, the goat boy, and the doctor who has come from Frankfurt to live in Dörfli. It must be a charming village."

"It is home," said Heidi simply.

"The school will be like home to you soon," the teacher assured her. "All our girls are very happy. You will not find the lessons difficult. Do you understand a little French?"

"They do not teach French in Dörfli," Heidi answered. "But the doctor has given me some instruction at home."

"Splendid! Then you'll get on."

Miss Smith led the way out of the station, followed by a porter carrying Heidi's things.

"We take a carriage here to drive up to the school. It is at Rosiaz, just above Lausanne, as Clara probably has told you."

"*Oui*, Mademoiselle," replied Heidi politely, thinking that now she must speak in French.

"My name is Miss Smith, and that is what you must call me," the teacher explained. "Be sure to pronounce the *th* in Smith by placing your tongue between your teeth. The students have a maddening way of calling me 'Miss Miss' because they won't take the trouble to pronounce it properly."

She helped Heidi up the high step into the carriage and sat down beside her.

As they drove on, the green fields called to Heidi's mind the green slope of the Alm and her grandfather, alone in his hut next to the pines. He would not be on the mountain long, she consoled herself. When the snows came he would go down, as usual, and live with the doctor and his neighbors in Dörfli. For the once embittered old Alm-Uncle had become endeared to the villagers for his increasing thoughtfulness and care of the orphan, Heidi. As a little child, she had been literally dumped on him by her Aunt Dete when a fine position had been offered the woman and she found the daughter of her sister, Adelheid, too much of a care. Heidi had been christened Adelheid, for her mother, but nobody ever thought of calling her by that name except the stern Fräulein Rottenmeier when Heidi had lived with Clara in Frankfurt. She hoped now that none of the teachers at Rosiaz would be like Fräulein Rottenmeier. Certainly Miss Smith was different, determined as she was to be pleasant and talkative. Heidi sat in her corner of the carriage only half-listening as the teacher rattled on. She switched from one subject to another with alarming rapidity. Her ancestors . . . it seemed that one of them came from Milan. . . . Mademoiselle, the headmistress, who was kind but firm . . . Clara . . . Mops . . . a perfect jumble of kindly chatter which left poor Heidi quite bewildered.

"Mops is so affectionate. Mademoiselle will like him very much. He has never bitten anyone yet," she finished unexpectedly just as Heidi was thinking that "Mops" seemed a very odd name for a professor.

"Oh, he's a cat!" she said, light breaking over her face. "I'm glad there's a cat. We had kittens at Clara's."

At last they reached Hawthorn, as the school was called, and Heidi, still dazed by her long journey, Miss Smith's chatter, and the strangeness of everything around her, found herself in a large reception room where she was greeted by a very dignified lady of some fifty-odd years.

The woman spoke kindly in spite of her stern appearance.

"Welcome to Hawthorn, Heidi. We are very glad to have you with us. I hope that you had a pleasant journey and that you are going to give us as much satisfaction as your friend Clara. Are you hungry? Louise, the cook, has prepared some cold meat and fruit for you. What have you there under your arm? Ah! A violin. Your grandfather wrote me that you had learned to play. It seemed to please him very much. Here you will be placed in good hands for your violin lessons."

She turned to the English teacher. "Miss Smith, will you please show Heidi to her room and see that she has everything that is necessary. Good night, Heidi. Sleep well. The rising bell rings at seven in the morning."

"Good night," said Heidi timidly.

"You should say, 'Good evening, Mademoiselle,' " the headmistress corrected her at once.

Heidi looked from one strange face to another. "Miss" for the English teacher, "Mademoiselle" for the headmistress! And at home she had always been taught to call the schoolmistress "Fräulein." How would she ever get them straight?

Confused and tired, she followed Miss Smith down a long hall. The room which she was to share with a young English girl, Eileen, was on the second floor. All the other rooms were closed and quiet. Everyone seemed to be asleep.

"Walk softly, so as not to waken the girls. You can arrange your things tomorrow. Now, shall we go to the dining room?"

"Thank you, I am not hungry," said Heidi.

"You will take your meat and fruit as the mistress has directed," Miss Smith said firmly.

When Heidi had eaten what she could, they continued on up the stairs. Finally they reached the room. Heidi looked around in the dim light and saw two wooden beds, two washbowls, two closets, one table and two chairs . . . all glistening white. The room seemed very comfortable. But the moment Miss Smith closed the door a wave of homesickness swept over Heidi. In spite of all her courage, tears filled her eyes. She went to the window and very gently opened the shutters.

"Oh!" she exclaimed impulsively. "The lake! The mountains!"

Everything was calm, so calm it almost seemed like her own countryside. A full moon rode in the sky and traced a golden path across the water. Heidi blinked back her tears to see. Already she loved the lake and felt cheered because it was there.

The door opened without a sound and six curious heads peeked in.

"Come in. I am Heidi," said Heidi in a whisper. "Who are you?"

19

The six stole in on tiptoe and one dark girl stepped forward to introduce the others.

"This is Eva Muller from Hamburg," she said, presenting the blond German miss. "She is the tallest of us all and so we all respect her." She said this with a grimace as she hauled forward the next two. "Edith and Molly, two close friends who came together from England. Behind them is Jeanne-Marie, a Hungarian girl. We've shortened it to Jamy to fit her little person. And here is Mademoiselle Anne de Fauconnet. One of her ancestors, Gaeton, fought in the battle of Issus with Saint Louis in 6000 B.C."

"Oh, Lise! My ancestor was not named Gaeton. He never fought with Saint Louis and it wasn't in the year 6000 B.C. How can you say such things?" protested Anne laughingly. She was not a bit angry, for she had soon discovered that her roommate's constant teasing was all in good fun.

"And now for me," continued Lise. "I am Lise Brunet, Swiss, vaguely related to Mademoiselle the directress, who doesn't love me any better for it. When Eileen comes we shall be complete. Now tell us about yourself."

In a few words Heidi told them about her life with the grandfather high in the Alps and the time she had spent with Clara in Frankfurt.

"At Dörfli the schoolmistress was enthusiastic about my music, but when she left the new schoolmaster didn't want to be bothered teaching the violin. He was stern and hard. All he thought of was teaching the children what was necessary and keeping them in order. Grandfather could see I was not happy in such a school so he and my godfather, the doctor, decided to send me to Lausanne so that I might study with a good professor. I didn't want to go at first, and leave them, but they thought it best. They are so good to me."

"We shall be good to you, too," Lise assured her. "And now, back to bed. We'll see you tomorrow."

One after the other they slipped out. Jamy, the last, smiled so sweetly at Heidi that the newcomer forgot she was homesick and felt warm and happy again. Undressing quickly, she knelt to say her prayers.

"Dear God, thank you! Thank you for guiding me here!" was all she could say at first. Then she added softly, "Please help me to work so that when I go back to Dörfli I can make Grandfather proud of me. And please watch over him and watch over the doctor and the good pastor and his wife and all the villagers in Dörfli. Make the schoolmaster kind and the children happy. Bless the dear grandmother in heaven and watch especially over Brigitte and Peter, the goat general. Don't let the Turk butt him and don't let him go too near the edge of the cliff. And watch over Schwanli and Barli and Distelfinck and Schneehopli."

So, one by one, she named the goats until she was quite weary and lay down on her bed to sleep.

2

THE SUN, shining through the latticed windows, awakened Heidi before the rising bell. A busy day followed, filled with both pleasant and unpleasant happenings.

Heidi met the French teacher, Mademoiselle Raymond, who was very long and thin and nearsighted. She wore a high collar and a high knot of hair on the top of her head and there was a row of buttons that paraded down her back like so many small beetles. She stooped down to look at Heidi and murmured, "I am very strict, especially about dictation. Your friend Clara learned well, very well indeed."

Heidi began to be afraid she could not live up to Clara, of whom everyone in the school had such a good opinion. She felt even more convinced of this when she talked to Fräulein Feld.

"Good morning, Heidi! I hope we shall be a happy family and that you are going to be as gay and lovable as your friend. Clara had such a delightful disposition."

She said this to impress Heidi with the importance of good behavior, but privately Fräulein Feld felt a very real sympathy for this simple fourteen-year-old country girl with her two long braids and her plain cotton dress. How would her classmates receive her? All of them were girls of good families and more or less well-to-do. Fräulein Feld was not in the habit of betraying her inner feelings, however, so she merely shrugged her shoulders and said aloud, "Well, we shall see. . . ."

That first morning Heidi made fifty-two errors in the dictation about which Mademoiselle Raymond was so very strict. She did not understand one of Fräulein's orders in gym class and she made a spot on the spotless tablecloth at luncheon.

Mademoiselle Larbey, the headmistress, gave her a very severe look.

"We are not living in a village," she said. "You must learn to eat properly."

"Excuse me, Mademoiselle," said Heidi. "It was an accident."

"Do not answer back when I correct you. It's impertinent," said the directress.

Heidi, who had not meant to be rude, sat silent and confused.

Mademoiselle Larbey resumed. "This afternoon you will take a walk with Miss Smith. At four thirty, after Eileen has arrived, I shall meet you in the study room and read aloud the rules of the school. Be especially kind to Eileen, girls. Her father has just died at Buenos Aires where he was Consul General, and her mother is ill."

After the walk, Heidi went to her room and found Eileen, the new pupil, in a flurry of dresses, hats, slippers, books, gloves, and suitcases.

"How do you do, Eileen. I am Heidi, your roommate."

"How do you do," Eileen replied stiffly, not bothering to raise her head.

"May I help you with your things?" Heidi offered, remembering that the headmistress had asked the girls to be especially kind.

"No, thank you. I would much rather have this room to myself. Couldn't you ask to be changed?" Eileen demanded.

"I'm afraid not," Heidi told her. "The other girls have been here longer than I. They already have roommates."

"How annoying!" And Eileen turned her back unsociably as she continued unpacking her suitcases.

On the balcony Heidi found Jamy, Lise, Anne, and Eva.

"Eileen is here," she announced.

"Yes? What is she like?" asked Lise.

"Tall, thin, with very black hair and green eyes," said Heidi.

"Is she nice?" asked Jamy.

"Go in and see for yourselves and then tell me what you think of her," Heidi responded.

The four girls disappeared through the long French doors leading into the room.

"Hello, Eileen!" they said.

"Oh, hello! Why am I in the same room with that little peasant girl?" the new girl stormed.

"But that's Heidi!" protested Lise.

"Who is *Heidi?*" demanded Eileen.

"Clara's friend," spoke up Eva.

"The granddaughter of the Alm-Uncle up in the mountains," added Anne.

"She plays the violin beautifully," said Jamy.

"Then she is an artist . . . a peasant and an artist . . . how dreadful! Why couldn't I have a room with you?" asked Eileen, turning toward Anne, whose cultured French background made her quite distinguished-looking.

"Impossible! Since I came three days ago I've been afflicted with the companionship of Lise here. We argue all the day long," she went on with a laugh, "but I wouldn't leave her for the world."

"What a pity! And you?" persisted Eileen, turning to Eva.

"Me?" asked Eva, somewhat taken aback. "I'm very happy rooming with Jamy. I'm big and she's little so we balance each other perfectly. Anyway, Heidi is very nice and we all like her."

"She doesn't please me," said Eileen majestically.

"That's just too bad," concluded Lise. But she left the room with a merry twinkle in her eyes. Heidi had been attacked and they had all had an opportunity to defend her.

On one side of the classroom where the new students gathered to hear the solemn reading of the rules, a large door opened on a beautifully kept garden. While they were waiting for Mademoiselle Larbey to come, Heidi slipped out to look at the little clusters of primroses in the short grass, the fat buds on the horse-chestnut trees which were just beginning to open and show bits of wrinkled leaves, and a little woolly cloud floating overhead, which seemed to have drifted over from the mountains. It looked like Schneehopli (Snow-hopper), the little white orphan goat that had been Heidi's favorite when she first went up to the pasture with Peter.

"Heidi! Here she comes!" warned one of the girls.

Heidi just had time to slip back into her place when Mademoiselle Larbey marched in.

The directress began to read in a solemn voice:

" 'Rules of Hawthorn School:

'One: Politeness is the rule at all times.

'Two: At half past nine all lights are to be out.

'Three: You are forbidden to play the piano when the windows are open.

'Four: You are not permitted to hang pictures or photographs on the wall.

'Five: You are forbidden . . .

'Six: You must not . . .

'Seven: Students must . . .

'Eight: Young girls must not . . .' "

and so, on and on, for two long pages. Then there were enumerations of penalties: no promenade, fines of from ten centimes to one franc, room confinement, parents notified, dismissal.

All the students were much impressed and looked at one another in silence after the headmistress had left the room. But Lise, more mischievous than the rest, saved the situation by remarking in the pedantic manner of Mademoiselle Larbey, "Above all, it is forbidden to take those rules too seriously."

The girls were all laughing when Mademoiselle Raymond came into the room. She hushed them with a lifted finger.

"Go to work, now," she said reproachfully. "You, Lise, to the piano. Heidi, Monsieur Rochat is here to give you your first lesson on the violin. Eileen, you may go and tidy your room. Anne and Eva will have a lesson in English and the rest of you will study with me."

Monsieur Rochat took a fatherly interest in Heidi and asked her many questions about her life in Dörfli. To these she responded with frankness and simplicity, as was her custom. Then he, in turn, told her about the mountains which he knew and loved. He passed his vacation in the Alps every year acting as guide for the students of the school when they went climbing.

"How long have you been playing the violin?" he asked Heidi.

"For two years," she replied.

"And who first gave you the idea of playing?" he continued, feeling a growing interest in his new pupil.

"First the murmur of the wind in the pines high up on the mountain, and then Clara gave me a violin," said Heidi.

"Good! Now let us see what you can do."

Heidi wanted so much to please the new teacher that her fingers were all thumbs and she played very badly.

"My child," he said, "you have a long way to go before you become an accomplished musician."

"The violin didn't sound like that when I played it up on the Alm," said Heidi, looking at the instrument in perplexity.

"The violin is all right," her music teacher told her.

"It is only the girl who feels the strangeness of her surroundings."

"When I look at the lake," said Heidi, "I do not feel strange anymore."

"Then play by the window, child."

"Indeed I will!" cried Heidi, rushing to open the shutters. "Now I will play for the grandfather and the good doctor and Brigitte and Peter up in the mountains. I will even play for the blind grandmother in her garden most fair."

"And where is that?" gently asked her teacher.

"Where the blind see," said Heidi devoutly. "The grandmother used to tell me about it when I read hymns to her, and then I learned to play for her and it made her happy. But now she hears only heavenly music."

"What a sweet faith," murmured Monsieur Rochat, taking out a large handkerchief to wipe his eyes. Then he said with confidence, "You will play, Heidi. But you will always play best for those who most need your music."

While Heidi Was Away

3

IT WAS SPRINGTIME in Dörfli. Purple and white crocuses bloomed along the slopes, the paths were edged with coltsfoot, and the music of busy little brooklets sounded everywhere.

This morning when the Alm-Uncle looked up to the high mountain peaks, the last patch of white snow on the road had disappeared.

"Doctor, tomorrow we shall go up on the mountain, the goats and I," he announced happily.

"You're not seriously thinking of going up so soon, Uncle. I am in no position to advise you, but you are no longer young. Why not stay here and trust your goats to Peter?" asked his friend.

"Ah, Doctor," sighed the old man, "you don't understand that I *must* go, and all the more because it will probably be the last time. I need to be up there to think and meditate. I feel nearer to God."

"But wait a little," urged the doctor. "The evenings are still cool and the nights are cold."

"I've seen many like them, my dear friend," replied the uncle. "Thank you all the same, but the mountains call me and tomorrow I shall go."

Knowing that it was useless to insist further, the doctor said no more. But he looked anxiously after the old man as he went off to make his preparations for departure.

After a moment of hesitation, the good doctor went in search of Peter. He found him attempting to repair a hole in the roof of his mother's hut where the wind had blown a piece of the covering away. Peter was clumsy with his hands and knew it well. Another winter, he said, and there would be no hut left.

"The uncle used to fix it," he complained.

"Peter, the uncle is old," the doctor told him. "The chill winds up on the Alm can do him no good. Nevertheless, he is determined to go up the mountain tomorrow with his goats. What can we do to stop him?"

"Nothing," said Peter resignedly.

"Nothing! Do you want the old man to freeze?"

"No," the boy replied. "I only know it is impossible to change him. But you will be left alone?"

"I will, indeed," the doctor replied, "unless you and your good mother will forsake this hut and keep my house in order for me."

Peter looked dubiously at the roof he was trying to

fix. He might lay on boards and more boards and cover them over with tar paper and gravel, but it was no use, because the foundations of the house were rotting away and his nails no longer held the decaying wood together. Yes, he decided, it was useless to try to repair it. Brigítte would be happy making her cakes and loaves for the doctor. He would enjoy eating them at the doctor's table where, so often, he had sat and talked with Heidi.

"We will come," he announced, sliding down from the roof.

"Splendid! But first you must help the uncle with his luggage. It is much too heavy for him to carry alone. Only," he added, "don't tell him that."

Peter understood. The Alm-Uncle grew melancholy when he realized his strength was failing. That afternoon Peter loitered around the house in Dörfli.

"May I come with you to milk the goats, Uncle?" he asked as soon as the old man appeared.

"Good day, goat general. Surely, come along," said the Alm-Uncle good-humoredly.

"Your goats look as though they'd had a bath," remarked the boy when the animals were led from the stable.

"They must be clean to greet the sun, Peter," the old man replied. "The sun has taken the trouble to prepare a new mountain for us with fresh green grass and bright little flowers, and a clean hut washed by the snow. The goats and I cannot go up there tomorrow and put the sun to shame."

"I would like to come with you tomorrow. May I?"

"What about school?" said the uncle.

"Will you never remember that I have finished school? Anyway, tomorrow is Sunday," Peter added quickly.

"All right," the old man replied, "if it will make you happy, you may come."

On the following morning the little hut on the Alm opened wide its doors and windows as if to drink up the early sunshine. Days went by. The warmth of the spring sun woke up first the little blue gentians—those with a white star in the center; then, one by one, all the other lovely flowers opened their petals. There were jonquils and red primroses and little golden rockroses with thorns on the edge of their petals. They all bloomed in their brightest colors while Peter watched the miracle taking place, as he had watched it every spring since he could remember. He had never quite seen the beauty of it, however, until Heidi had come to show him.

The grass in the pasture became glistening and sweet, spreading a feast for the frolicsome goats. Peter was up with the sun every morning and, in the evening when he came down the mountainside, he always found the uncle waiting for him.

"Have you seen the hawk, general?" the old man

asked anxiously one evening.

"Yes, Uncle," Peter replied. "I have seen it often."

"Has it succeeded in getting a kid?"

"No, Uncle. I am strong, you know," said Peter. "If the hawk comes too close to the herd, I hit at him with my stick and throw rocks at him. He is wise enough to keep away."

"You are more brave than Gerard, the goatherd from Ragatz. I have often seen the hawk pick a young kid from his flock. But with whom do you talk up there in the pasture?"

"You are making fun of me, Uncle," said Peter.

"But no," he replied. "I, too, am alone all day. I, too, enjoy a good chat in the evening. If Heidi were here, she'd go with you. Then you would not be alone with the goats and the hawk. She liked so much going up to the pasture."

Schwanli and Barli, the two goats belonging to the Alm-Uncle, felt the sadness in his voice and pushed their noses close to him as if to say, "We are here; we are here. Now you are not alone."

The uncle stroked them and gave them some salt.

"Heidi would like to feed the goats again," he sighed.

Peter scratched his close-cropped, curly hair, trying to think of something to say to distract the grandfather and turn his thoughts in a more cheerful direction. But all his talk about the bright flowers that were blooming in the pasture, about the sweet grass, and about the frisking goats brought forth the same reply: "Heidi would like to see them."

Tuesday was a particularly happy day for the Alm-Uncle. On that day Peter hurried up the mountain, holding fast in his hand the letter which Heidi wrote every Sunday. At the boarding school one could not write whenever one wished, but only on Sunday.

Up before the sun, the grandfather often walked halfway down to meet the goatherd. He did not read the letter at once, but waited until he was comfortably seated on his bench in front of the hut. Here he had a view of the whole valley. He felt that he could thus reach out in thought to Heidi, while gazing down the road which twines between mountains as far as Lausanne.

Dear Grandfather (said the letter), I am working as hard as I can in order to come home as quickly as possible. Monsieur Rochat is pleased and so is Mademoiselle Raymond, though she pretends that I cannot pronounce my "r's" correctly. Please kiss Schwanli and Barli for me. Kiss them real hard, right on their noses, and don't forget to give some salt to Distelfinck when Peter goes by with the herd. She always looks so slender, as if she needed strength.

I often worry about you, up there in the hut alone. And I wish, so much, that I could be with you. This evening when you are sitting outside on your bench, listen to the wind as it rushes through the tops of the trees, and think of me. I'll be, at that moment, in the little turret room playing the violin for Monsieur Rochat. But I'll imagine that I am in the hut with you, and it will be as though I am playing for you.

The letter continued for three more pages with a whole list of things the grandfather was supposed to attend to in the hut. Heidi also wished him to gather some mountain flowers, dry them, and send them to her so that she might decorate her room in the same way she had decorated her little loft bedroom at home. She said she liked the boarding school. She liked her work and her companions. But the grandfather read a great deal of homesickness between the lines of her letter, as well as a great deal of cheerfulness of spirit.

The grandfather read Heidi's letter over and over again during the entire week. He would meditate over it, sentence by sentence, delighted when his little girl was happy, depressed when he thought she seemed sad.

Peter was not pleased. The grandfather's face was beginning to take on a gray look. His eyes had lost their twinkle. One Tuesday the grandfather did not come to meet him as usual and Peter became alarmed. He rushed up to the hut, thinking surely something must have happened to him, but the old man was only sitting quietly on the bench, waiting for him to arrive.

"Are you bringing me the letter, general?"

"Yes, Uncle," Peter replied. "But you look tired. Is anything wrong?"

"Nothing is wrong and I am not tired," the Alm-Uncle said. "It is only because I am old."

"But you have been old a long time."

"Before I did not feel it. Now I do."

July came. The school in Dörfli had been closed for some time and now the grandfather observed every day crowds of youngsters climbing the slopes outside the village to help their parents with the haying. The grandfather had already, by himself, cut the grass behind the hut, had turned it over to dry, and had finally carried the hay on his back into the little barn. He had been sending Heidi letters that were short, but full of affection, and often had sent dried Alpine flowers. One day he said to Peter, "Take the goats a little higher than usual today. Take them to the right of the great rock where the grass is tender and sweet. Make sure that Schwanli and Barli get their fill of this grass. Their milk must be especially good as I'd like to make a little cheese for Heidi. Don't you think that is a good idea, general?"

Peter, who shared with the herdsman of antiquity a taste for good cheese, approved wholeheartedly.

"Oh, what a fine idea, Uncle!" he exclaimed. "Heidi will certainly be pleased."

A Present From the Grandfather

4

IT WAS NEARING the end of the term at school and some of the students were leaving for vacation. Lise was going to the country to spend a month with her parents. Anne was going home to Brittany. Eva was leaving with friends with whom she was going to pass her vacation in the mountains. But Eileen, Heidi, Jamy, and the two English girls were staying at school.

Now that Eva was gone, Heidi would have liked to share her room with Jamy, who had become her best friend, but she would not ask permission to change for fear of hurting Eileen.

One day, near the beginning of vacation, she received a little package from Dörfli, beautifully wrapped and tied with string. The girls were curious and tried to guess what it was.

"It's chocolate!"

"No, it's a round package."

"Perhaps it's a bunch of flowers. They'll be quite withered."

"All wrong! I'm sure it's a cake."

"Hurry, Heidi," they all begged. "Open it and see who's right."

Heidi cut the string and opened the package. To the astonishment of all the other girls, there lay a little goat cheese, round and white.

"Cream cheese!" they exclaimed, wrinkling their noses.

"It smells bad," one of the English girls added. "Poor Heidi! Your grandfather must have thought you were starving!"

"It's a good joke," they all agreed, beginning to giggle. Heidi alone did not laugh. For a moment she wished she might throw the unfortunate cheese out of the window because they were all making fun of her. Then she felt instantly ashamed of herself. In her mind she saw the little hut on the Alm and her grandfather working over the copper kettle. She remembered how willingly she had climbed on the little chair he had made for her when she heard the call to supper. And usually there was nothing but coarse bread and cheese and goat's milk to wash it down. How hungrily she and Peter had eaten cheeses like this when they climbed together to tend his flock up on the mountain! The grandfather's two goats, Schwanli and Barli, had given of their best milk to make it and the grandfather himself had stirred it to a snowy consistency with his great wooden spoon. Now Heidi confessed to a yearning for the familiar taste of cheese.

"You are welcome to it!" her schoolmates teased her.

Laughing and joking, they left the room, holding their noses.

"Phew! What a smell!"

"Quick, some air!"

"Throw open a window and let the wind do its worst!"

"I don't want to stay in that room. She'll probably keep her cheese for a souvenir and I can't stand that odor!" cried Eileen.

Everybody stopped laughing. Edith, so polite, elegant, refined that everyone copied her, looked at Eileen in surprise.

"But, Eileen, you are not serious, I hope. We were only joking."

"Oh, *you* can talk! Heidi isn't in *your* room," said Eileen.

"If I weren't with Molly, whom I have known for so long, I would love to room with Heidi," said Edith warmly.

"Well, not I," snapped Eileen. "I have had enough of her. I am going to ask Mademoiselle Larbey to change my room."

"You wouldn't!"

"I certainly would. Just see!"

The study bell rang and cut short the commotion. In spite of its being vacation time the students worked every day between five and six thirty. They all marched to their classes looking as if something unpleasant had happened. Heidi looked especially sad when she entered the music room where Monsieur Rochat was waiting for her.

"What is the matter, Heidi?" he asked with deep concern. "Have you received bad news from Dörfli?"

"Thank you, no," replied Heidi. "Grandfather and the doctor are well and Peter and his mother are very happy in the doctor's house."

"Then it must be here that something is wrong," persisted her teacher.

"No, everything is all right," said Heidi.

Monsieur Rochat questioned her no more, but he resolved to find out what had happened. He was very fond of Heidi and could not bear to see her looking sad without knowing the reason.

After class he went to the library as usual to wait until it was time for dinner. There he found a group of teachers talking excitedly and wagging their heads at one another. Now he was sure that something had happened. But what?

"It's unthinkable," the headmistress was saying in a shocked tone. "One would suppose that my students were starving, that I did not give them enough to eat. What will everyone think of my school? I do not know what to do." She wrung her hands quite tragically.

"What must one do?" Miss Smith asked, equally tragic.

Something was displayed on the library table. They were all scrutinizing it, but the professor, from his corner, failed to see what it was.

"The question, it seems to me," remarked Mademoiselle Raymond, "is not so much what to do with this . . . this outrage, as what to do with Eileen. She does not wish to room with Heidi anymore."

"Ah! And I can well understand it," the headmistress sighed. "A child so delicate, so sensitive! What is *your* opinion of all this, Miss Smith? What room can we give Heidi? Of course it's perfectly clear that no one will want to stay with a little peasant who harbors goat cheese in her room."

Monsieur Rochat had listened thus far without comprehending. Now he understood. His mouth twitched a little, but still he said nothing.

"It's impossible to sleep in the same room with Heidi," the English teacher gave out as her opinion, "if she insists on keeping that cheese. It would not be healthy."

"But anyway," interrupted Fräulein Feld, "she is not responsible for the extraordinary gift."

The music professor had come a little closer, his

mouth still twitching under his heavy moustache.

"And you, Monsieur Rochat, what do you think?" asked the principal at last.

"I have nothing to say, at least for the moment," he replied.

"Have Jamy, Edith, and Molly come in and we will try to arrange something," said Mademoiselle Larbey, after a pause.

Fräulein hurried to call them. They were all three in the English girls' room having a heated discussion.

"Mesdemoiselles," began the principal when Fräulein had brought the girls to the library, "you know what has happened. Your schoolmate Eileen has refused to room with Heidi. Would one of you mind rooming with Eileen?"

For a moment there was complete silence. Then Edith raised her eyes and said, "Mademoiselle, we would all three like to share a room with *Heidi!*" And she stressed the name, "Heidi."

Then Jamy spoke up. "Molly and Edith are friends. While Eva is away on vacation, I am alone. Could Heidi please move in with me?"

"We will decide that later," said the directress, a little disconcerted. "You may go now."

She turned to Monsieur Rochat, who had been enjoying the little scene immensely. "You see, I had my reasons for not intervening. Everything has arranged itself beautifully," he said.

"You may think so," she retorted, "but *nothing* is arranged. What am I going to tell Eileen? She will be heartbroken, poor child!" the directress added with a stiff attempt at sympathy.

"Possibly, but it will do her good," replied the professor. "Doesn't anyone think of Heidi's heart?"

The teachers looked at one another, confused, and the professor left the library chuckling to himself.

When he met Heidi at dinner Monsieur Rochat called her aside and spoke to her gently. "I hear you have received a specialty from Dörfli, a beautiful little goat cheese. May we not taste it? I am sure your chums have never eaten it and, as for me, it is not often I have such a treat."

Heidi blushed and looked at the girls who were sitting at her table. Everywhere she saw smiles of encouragement, and once more Edith spoke for the others.

"Do please let us try it, Heidi," she begged.

Everyone, except Eileen, who wouldn't touch it, ate a piece of the "specialty from Dörfli." Some thought it delicious, while others did their best to pretend to like it.

Heidi knew when they were merely being polite by the tone of their voices, and she smiled to see Molly's face as she courageously finished her piece.

After dinner Mademoiselle Larbey joined the girls in the sitting room.

"Eileen," she said, "we have decided to let you have

a room alone. Not one of the girls in your class wished to share it with you. They all expressed their willingness, however, to room with Heidi. It seems to me that this is something which you will understand better if you think it over by yourself. I will talk with you later on the subject in my office. You may come at eight thirty. As for you, Heidi, you may move into Jamy's room and take what's left of your little goat cheese with you."

"Oh, thank you, Mademoiselle!" Heidi exclaimed gratefully.

"Heidi!"

"Jamy!" cried Heidi as the two girls embraced. She could say no more, but her eyes were like lakes, shining with happy tears.

A Letter to the Directress

5

WHEN THE DOCTOR met Peter in the village he asked for news of the Alm-Uncle up on the mountain.

"He is very sad," sighed Peter.

"Sad, why?" asked the doctor, surprised. "What makes you think he is sad?"

"He is sad because he is lonely," said Peter simply.

"But that is just what he wanted!" exploded the doctor. "Don't you think I did everything I could to keep him from going up to that hut alone?"

"He is sad because he misses Heidi," Peter added.

"How do you know that?" demanded the doctor.

"Because I know it," Peter replied.

"That is no answer," the doctor said impatiently. "Look here, just exactly what is wrong?"

Peter thought a moment before he answered. "The

uncle never laughs. He just sits on his bench and when I go by with the goats he says, 'Heidi would like to go up on the mountain with you today.' Sometimes he says, almost to himself, 'It seems it is best she should not come . . . but I am not sure.' "

"Thank you, Peter. I shall go to see him myself."

Next morning, about ten o'clock, when the doctor reached the hut, the bench was empty. Perhaps the Alm-Uncle was in the back mending some of his tools. But he was not there, either. Feeling anxious, the doctor went into the kitchen and what he saw made him stop short in the doorway. The old man was seated before the table, his head bowed over on his folded arms. He seemed to be sleeping.

"Good morning, Uncle. You didn't hear me come in," said the doctor. "I hope I haven't disturbed you."

"Oh, my friend! So it's you?" cried the Alm-Uncle, straightening himself. "You are good to come all the way up here. Any news of our little girl this week?" And he began again on Heidi, his favorite topic. "Did she tell you about her last adventure? She writes that all the girls went to the city and stopped before a shop window to look at a painting of the mountains. Heidi was so absorbed in the picture that she did not hear Mademoiselle Raymond call, and suddenly she found she was alone. But instead of returning directly to school, she confessed she stayed on looking at the painted mountains because they reminded her of home.

Then she walked alone all around the town. She gets those independent ideas from Schwanli and Barli, but I am glad that she is not afraid to find her way about alone, even in the city. I have her last letter right here," he added, pulling it from his pocket and laying it on the table. "It seems she loves the sewing class and is looking forward to teaching the young girls of Dörfli how to sew. She might use the large room in your house, Doctor, for her class . . . that large room under the roof which is not being used for anything. What do you think?"

Just the mere thought of Heidi made his old eyes sparkle with happiness. He was proud of his granddaughter's intelligence and her spirit of independence. Now he glanced up mischievously at the doctor, sure of his approval.

"Transform my laboratory into a sewing room!" exclaimed the doctor. "And I, where shall I go with my bottles and test tubes? Perhaps she expects me to learn to sew, too, under her expert direction! Children are a great trial, Uncle. Now I shall have to move down to the cellar."

They talked for hours about Heidi's proposed sewing class, about her music, and about the friends she had made in the school. The grandfather's eyes were bright as they talked, but when the doctor rose to go he again looked dejected.

"I would stay longer," his friend told him, "but it

51

is already four o'clock and I promised to see old Seppeli this afternoon. He is nearing the end."

"We are the same age, Seppeli and I," mused the
Alm-Uncle. "We were both just twenty years old when
we first met down in the valley. . . ."

It seemed as though he had more to say, but he
stopped short, lost in thought. Perhaps he was thinking
of his wasted youth, his parents long gone, or of the
many years he had spent as a hermit alone on the mountain before Heidi came to him. After a long silence, he
began again in a low voice. "Yes, we are the same age
and you say he is ready to die!"

And now the doctor understood all that was passing
through the old man's mind.

After he had made his call on old Seppeli, the doctor
hurried home to his desk and wrote the following
letter:

Chere Mademoiselle:

I had intended leaving my goddaughter Heidi
at school for the vacation so that she might continue her music lessons. I find now that I must
change my plans. Her grandfather misses her very
much. He is well on in years and I do not feel I
have the right to deprive him of his beloved grand-
child any longer. Therefore I would like to have
you make the necessary arrangements for Heidi to
come to Dörfli for the month of August. I am too

busy to fetch her myself and I would be grateful if you will have someone come with her as far as Maienfeld, if not all the way to Dörfli.

I know that Heidi is very fond of her young friend Jamy, and it would give us pleasure to have her as our guest for several weeks. You know me well enough to recommend me to her parents. I would appreciate your cooperation in sending the girls to us as soon as possible.

With kind regards, I am

Very sincerely yours,

Doctor Reboux

The letter reached the school Saturday evening by the five o'clock mail. Heidi was waiting at the gate with Jamy when the postman came.

"Is there anything for me?" she asked.

Ever since the others had left for vacation the mailman had been more friendly. Perhaps he felt a little sorry for those who had to remain at school. So, against the strict orders of Mademoiselle Larbey, he showed the girls the bunch of letters directed to the school.

"A letter from my godfather, the doctor! And it's addressed to the principal! That's strange, and nothing for me!" exclaimed Heidi, recognizing the well-known handwriting.

"A postcard from Mama," said Jamy. "She is at the seashore with some friends . . . her friends, not mine."

After a little silence, Jamy went on. "It is nice of her to send me a picture of the hotel, no doubt the nicest one there. She has plans for the fall and cannot come to see me. But it doesn't matter. I'm used to it by now."

But she spoke in a very small, halting voice that could not conceal her hurt feelings. Heidi, who was thinking about the other letter and only half-listening to Jamy, raised her head, suddenly aware of her friend's tone. Jamy never spoke of her family and Heidi knew only that her father was in the diplomatic service.

"What's the matter, Jamy?" she asked. "If your mother can't come it must be because she has something very important to attend to. You will most likely see her at Christmastime."

"No," replied Jamy. "Then she'll have another excuse not to come and I shall leave for England next year without a visit home and without having seen a single one of my family, neither my father nor my little sister."

Heidi was perplexed. Was it possible to have a mama and not a mother? Was it possible to be without a mother's love and yet not be an orphan? Heidi knew how it felt to be unloved because of the few lonely years she had spent with Aunt Dete before she was finally brought to the grandfather. It meant having no one to notice whether or not you ate; no one to see if your eyes were red, or if you didn't look well; no one to hear you coughing and be worried about you; no one to talk lovingly to you, to come to your room and open the shutters and lean over your bed and kiss you good night; to understand that in spite of your fourteen years you are still a little girl who needs love and protection. Poor Jamy! Perhaps there was no one in the whole world who was particularly interested in her, and maybe that was the reason why she was so often sad.

Heidi put her arm affectionately around her friend's neck and said warmly, "Jamy, I'm staying in school for the vacation, too. I've prayed that I might go home but, long ago, I found out that the dear Lord knows when it's best not to answer our prayers. Now I am glad that I must stay."

"But why, Heidi?"

"You need me here," Heidi replied. "You'd have no one to do things with if it weren't for me. But together we can have a wonderful time. We can take trips to the mountain with Monsieur Rochat. First we'll go to the Rocks of Naye and spend the night at the chalet of Sauaodoz so as to be there early in the morning to see the sunrise. You don't know how beautiful it is when the mountains are all aglow! And we'll find all kinds of wild flowers. Then we'll cross the lake in a little steamboat and climb up the Oche's Tooth. Monsieur Rochat might even take us to the Hospice of Saint Bernard, and we can see the mementos of Napoleon's march across the mountain with his army. Monks live way up there all the year around, with those big dogs that go out in the deep snow to rescue lost travelers. They have saved many people who ventured across the high peak. Then there are lots of other things to see, the salt pits at Bex, the fairy grotto of Saint Maurice. You just see if we don't have a beautiful summer without once being homesick!"

Heidi was so enthusiastic about it all that Jamy caught her spirit and was quite cheered.

"What is the fairy grotto?" she asked.

"It's like a large corridor in the mountain leading to an underground lake. Monsieur Rochat told me about it. The entrance is very small and narrow. You reach it by climbing a steep hill above the Rhone River, and there is a little house perched way up there for the nuns, and there is a guide to take you through. They give you a lamp to light your way along the dark passage," said Heidi.

"And the fairies?" asked Jamy.

"You can't see them, but you can hear them," Heidi told her mysteriously. "They have a room deep in the mountain and no one knows where it leads. If you put your ear against the wall you can hear the sound of a drum. They say it is a warning to those who are too curious and want to enter their retreat. Monsieur Rochat heard it quite distinctly."

"Do you believe in fairies, Heidi?" asked Jamy, who had quite recovered her spirits by this time.

"Not exactly, but Grandfather knows a great many

legends and folk tales and I love to hear them."

"Oh, I love legends, too," echoed Jamy.

"Maybe sometime you can come to Dörfli to visit me and then you can hear the legends, too."

"You aren't going to live in Dörfli all your life, are you?" asked Jamy, looking at her in great surprise.

"Why not?" Heidi wanted to know.

"You'd get lonesome after a while and feel shut in from the rest of the world . . . like a monk or nun."

"Shut in on those mountains! Never!" cried Heidi. "There's nothing in all the world that makes me so happy as going up on the mountains with Peter while he tends his goats. You may think me odd, Jamy. But when you've found something like that, you don't lose it. You keep it for the rest of your life."

"But just going up to the mountains," Jamy protested. "It isn't . . . *useful*. What will you do with your education?"

"I'll give it away," Heidi replied lightly. "I'll teach all the children in Dörfli everything I've learned here in Lausanne—how to sew and cook and knit, perhaps even how to paint pictures and play the violin. Oh, you'll see! I shall not be idle. I may even send for you to come and help me."

"I'd love to come—anyway, for a while," said Jamy. "But I don't believe Papa would want me to stay there. His ideas are all about social life and meeting the right people. He expects me to help him at the embassy when

I have learned to speak French and English well. And then you will come to visit me at Budapest, Vienna, or Berlin. Maybe even in Paris or London."

"Perhaps," said Heidi doubtfully. "Monsieur Rochat said I must go to Paris if I mean to continue my studies with the violin, but I'm not at all sure I want to go to Paris when those I love best are in Dörfli."

Good News

6

WHILE HEIDI AND JAMY were still talking at the gate, Mademoiselle Raymond appeared at the other end of the path and called to Heidi, waving her hands to beckon to her, but without raising her voice. She never raised her voice no matter what happened.

"Heidi! Heidi! Where are you? Ah, there you are!" She came over to the gate and asked, with great concern, "Heidi, is your village very high? Does one go up by foot or on mules? How many hours does it take to travel up from Maienfeld?"

"For you, Mademoiselle, it would take about eight hours," replied Jamy.

"Jamy, don't be impudent!" scolded the teacher. "Heidi, answer me!"

"Excuse me, Mademoiselle," said Jamy softly. "Heidi

and I were just talking about our plans for the vacation here and I felt especially gay."

"I think it would take two or three hours on foot," Heidi told her.

"On foot, you say!" cried Mademoiselle Raymond. "There must be an easier way."

"Yes," said Heidi. "You can take the mail cart at Maienfeld."

"There is a mail cart? Why didn't you say so at once? Thank heaven for that!"

Mademoiselle Raymond sighed, much relieved. Meanwhile Heidi waited, filled with curiosity, for her to explain. When she saw the teacher turn on her heel without a word, she ran after her, calling politely, "Excuse me, Mademoiselle, but may I know why you asked me all those questions?"

"Do you mean to spend your vacation at Dörfli?" laughed Jamy.

"Heaven forbid! You are very naughty today, Jamy. You take a positive pleasure in teasing me," scolded the old-maid teacher. "It may be necessary for me to travel to Dörfli, and I am not as young as you are."

Jamy felt immediately ashamed of her mischief and said no more, but Heidi was burning with impatience and curiosity.

"Why may you be obliged to travel to Dörfli?" she questioned. "Has anything happened to my grandfather? Is anybody ill?"

"Do not worry, my child. Your grandfather and your godfather and your friends in Dörfli, so far as I know, are well. I did not mean to alarm you," the teacher added.

"But what has happened?" persisted Heidi.

"Mademoiselle Larbey will tell you when she considers it time for you to know." And with that she left them as mystified and puzzled as ever.

"Jamy, what do you make of it?" demanded Heidi.

"Nothing good," said Jamy. "It seems to me that they have sent for you to go home. It looks as if our plans are spoiled and I shall have to stay here all summer."

"Do you really think that is what my godfather wrote to the principal about?" asked Heidi.

"I am sure. Mademoiselle Raymond is probably going to have to take you there, and that's why she is so worried. I hope you have a nice vacation," said Jamy wistfully.

Heidi was silent. She longed to see her grandfather and the doctor. She knew Peter had missed her and would be waiting for her to go again with him and his goats up on the mountainside. But she did not want to leave Jamy. Poor Jamy, with no one except herself to care whether she had a nice time or not! Heidi took her hand and together they walked back to the school building. Heidi found, when she went for her practice hour on the violin, that the music had a sad, sweet tone.

It was as though the mountains and the lake both were calling her . . . Jamy and her own people calling together.

"You are playing very well," Monsieur Rochat told her.

But Heidi felt she was not playing at all . . . it was only the violin. She was still under the spell of her own music that evening when Mademoiselle Larbey came to her and said, "My child, I have a message for you from your godfather. Will you come with me to my office?"

Jamy looked at her roommate as much as to say, "At last you are going to find out what was in that letter."

Heidi was quiet and subdued as she followed the directress down the long hall to her office. Ten minutes later she rushed out and quickly closed the door. Then she broke into a run. She tore down the hall and up the stairs like a mountain goat going over the rocks and, bursting into the room, she cried, "Jamy! Jamy! I am going to Dörfli for the month of August, and you, too! The doctor asked Mademoiselle Larbey and she telegraphed your father and he has given his permission. Isn't it wonderful? Where is my suitcase? What do I need to take? Nothing much, anyway, because I have more suitable clothes than these at home."

Jamy leaned against the wall as if stricken dumb. For a moment she could neither move nor speak. Heidi grabbed her by the shoulders and repeated, "You're coming with me, don't you understand? We are leaving tomorrow morning. Mademoiselle Raymond will take us all the way to Dörfli where the doctor will meet us. We'll probably spend the night at his house and then day after tomorrow morning we will go up to the grandfather on the mountain with Peter and the goats. But why don't you say something?" demanded Heidi at last. "Aren't you glad?"

"I am too happy to speak, dearest Heidi," said Jamy.

Before long Jamy found her voice again and nothing could stop her chatter. During the whole evening she and Heidi tried to out-talk one another while they packed their bags. If Jamy had listened to Heidi she would have taken only a few underclothes and a linen dress. It seemed that the people of Dörfli didn't wear shoes or hats or coats. Fortunately Mademoiselle Raymond superintended the packing. At ten thirty the bags were taken down to the hall and there was relative silence in the bedroom, though from time to time a murmur still came from one or the other of the beds.

"Did you think of your alpenstock?" or "Where did you put my bedroom slippers?" or "Will I find postal cards at Dörfli to send to Mama and Papa?"

At midnight everything was calm and still except for the soft breathing of the two girls. But everyone in the school was not asleep. In her little room under the roof, Mademoiselle Raymond lay wakeful and nervous. The headmistress had asked her to take the girls all the way to Dörfli. It would be impossible to return the same day and so she would probably have to spend the night there. To the poor woman this was a real calamity, a misfortune, almost a catastrophe. No longer young, she was terrified at the thought of keeping pace with two madcap girls. She remembered very well a trip to Simplon the year before, when she was drenched to the skin and shaking with cold. It was with a profound sigh that she had packed her heavy hobnail shoes, a large skirt, an ample cape, and a gray felt hat. She also planned to take an enormous umbrella. And she had carefully folded a woolen shawl, a flannel jacket, and a nightcap in her handbag—not that she ever wore a nightcap! But she intended to take no chances with the dangerous mountain air.

Home Again

7

IT WAS EARLY on a pleasant summer's evening that the two girls left the station at Maienfeld and took the narrow road which, starting at a gentle slope, became steeper and steeper as it approached Dörfli.

Mademoiselle Raymond, after all, was not undertaking the long climb. Having been assured that the girls would reach the little village before dark and would come to no harm on the way, she now sat in the station waiting thankfully for the next train back to Lausanne.

At the first bend in the road, Heidi and Jamy stopped to look at the splendid view. They could see the whole of Maienfeld, with its quaint, low houses, tall spires, and busy streets. A flock of geese was being driven home; oxcarts rumbled along the street. There were some fine carriages, driven by horses, and the distant whistle of the departing train could be heard as the engine sent a white cloud of smoke puffing in its wake all down the valley. Above the town were rich pastures filled with cattle and goats, then rocks and pine forests with more rocks and more pine forests above them.

"The view is not so gay from here," remarked Jamy as they climbed.

"Only wait!" Heidi told her.

As they climbed higher up, the air became sharper, perfumed with herbs and flowers. The meadows were gay with color. Then, at a turn in the road, they suddenly saw the Falknis, illuminated by the last rays of the sun. It towered above the other peaks, majestic and awe-inspiring as it reflected all the glorious brilliance of the sky on its snowcapped pinnacle. Heidi stopped in the middle of the path, and tears of joy came into her eyes at the sight of her beloved mountains.

"How beautiful it is!" Jamy cried. "Even the snow up there seems to be on fire. Now I understand your great love for the Alps, Heidi!"

They stood watching the sky until the splendor had faded. Now they realized how late it was growing and walked faster and faster, in order to reach the village before it became quite dark. Suddenly Jamy stopped, out of breath, and put her hand to her throat.

"Oh, Heidi!" she exclaimed. "I've lost something!"

"Your gold cross!" Heidi cried out, seeing that her neck was bare. Usually she wore a plain gold cross suspended from a narrow velvet ribbon which was knotted behind and worn quite thin. The ribbon apparently had broken, and now the cross was gone!

"I wouldn't have lost it for anything," wailed Jamy. "It belonged to my grandmother and she asked me always to keep it. She was kind to me, just as you say your grandfather is kind to you. But now she is gone and the cross was all I had to remember her by. Oh, what shall I do? My beautiful cross!"

And all at once Jamy was convulsed with sobs. She sat down on a rock that jutted out beside the path and cried as though her heart would break. Heidi tried to comfort her in vain and, although they looked and looked, they could not find the cross. They retraced their steps all the way back to Maienfeld, searching along the path. There they borrowed a little lantern and returned, still searching. But there was no trace either of the cross or the ribbon that had held it.

"It's no use," Jamy said at last. "It's gone and I'll never find it. I'll just not say anything more about it and try to have a nice vacation anyway."

Heidi's sympathy, this time, was wordless as they climbed back along the path. They were both feeling very tired and very depressed when suddenly, far above their heads, came the sound of joyous yodeling. The girls held up their lantern and looked, but could see no one, only the path zigzagging behind tall bushes and jutting rocks. Then a number of moving forms appeared among the bushes higher up, while the song rang out stronger and stronger.

"Look, Heidi! Oh, look! Here and over there! Oh! What is it?" cried Jamy, delighted, forgetting the lost locket and pointing excitedly.

Before Heidi could turn around, four goats bounded down the slope. Behind them others and still others came into view. Each one had a little bell around its neck and the tinkling sounded on all sides. Now the goatherd rounded the bend, dancing in the middle of a group of cavorting goats and singing, not in his native tongue, but in French and at the top of his lungs:

> "Way up on the mountain is a new chalet.
> For Jean, so brave and true,
> Has built it all a-new!
> Way up on the mountain is a new chalet. . . ."

After this came a ringing yodel. The singer skipped and jumped on his bare feet as lightly and swiftly as the capricious goats and in a moment had reached the spot where the girls stood.

"Good evening," he greeted them gaily, then paused to stare. But Heidi, who had recognized him first, made one leap and fell into his arms.

"Peter!"

"Heidi!" he exclaimed. "I never thought of meeting you here. My mother and the doctor were looking for you hours ago."

"We were late," Heidi began. But she saw Jamy

place her finger to her lips as much as to say, "Don't tell him. There's no use spoiling everything because of a lost locket."

"We were just late. And you, Peter?" she asked. "Why have you gone all the way down to Maienfeld?"

"I've added some new goats to my flock," the boy replied. "They belong to the schoolmaster and I'm bringing them up from his stable in Maienfeld. This little one is almost too small for the journey," he added, lifting a small, white kid to his arms and stroking its head. "Poor little Meckerli," he continued, talking to the goat. "Is the day too long for you? Is the mountain too steep?"

"What was it you called the little goat?" Jamy asked, coming closer to Peter.

"Meckerli," he replied. "It means 'Little One Who Bleats.' All the goats have names and all the names mean something."

"Heidi has told me of Schwanli and Barli [Little Swan and Little Bear], her grandfather's goats. Are they in your flock?"

"Not today," Peter replied. "But tomorrow, if you go up on the mountain with Heidi, you shall see them."

"I should love to go up!" Jamy exclaimed. "May I? And will you sing all of that lovely song about the chalet?"

"If Heidi will play the violin—"

"You know I will, Peter," she interrupted. "I taught

69

you the song, didn't I—when you and I were studying French with the doctor? And I always have played the violin whenever you asked me to."

"That was before you went away to school," he replied briefly.

"Pooh! Do you think I *wanted* to go away? It was only because the schoolmaster was so cruel. Peter," she asked anxiously, "has he changed?"

The boy shook his head.

"I don't suppose he ever will," said Heidi. "You see, Jamy," she continued, "I shall simply have to study hard and learn to teach the school myself."

When they reached Dörfli, Peter went first with his goats to see that they were stabled. But Heidi and Jamy ran on toward the house and arrived quite out of breath. The doctor was waiting for them in the doorway. He embraced Heidi tenderly and greeted Jamy with a friendly smile. Right away, Heidi wanted to know about her grandfather and was delighted to hear that he was well and that the doctor had planned her trip so that she might surprise him in the morning.

Brigitte had prepared a delicious supper of cheese and dried meat and they sat down to a gay meal. Peter came in with a fresh pitcher of goat's milk and set it down on the table.

"Come, Peterli," said his mother, "you must be hungry."

He sat down with them and helped himself to a

large slice of cheese. He said little during the meal. But Heidi had so much to tell about her life in school and all the little happenings of their trip with Mademoiselle Raymond that no one noticed his silence and the evening passed quickly.

Very early the next morning Jamy was awakened by a song echoing across the village square.

"It must be the goatherd!" she cried, jumping out of bed and running to the window where Heidi was already looking out. They saw Peter, his cheeks fresh and pink, coming up the path with his little troop beside him. He snapped his whip to bring the goats to a halt and set his horn to his lips. Already from the open doors of the stables other goats hurried out to join the herd.

"Hurry! Hurry, if you want to go up with the doctor and Peter. Hurry and dress!" cried Brigitte.

"We'll be ready right away," said Jamy, lacing her bodice. "I want the goatherd to sing his whole song for me today."

Ten minutes later the doctor, Jamy, and Heidi joined Peter and his flock, which now included all the goats from Dörfli.

He blew on his horn and they started on up the mountain. Rosy early morning clouds were still in the sky and the mountain air was fresh and sweet in their faces as they climbed. The higher they went, the more beautiful was the view. From time to time Peter stole a look at Heidi to see if the school had changed her and then smiled again in satisfaction to find that she was the same.

Everything was new to Jamy and she never once stopped asking questions about the eternal snows, the names of all the flowers, and especially about the eagles of which Heidi had so often spoken.

Suddenly they came up from a turn in the path and were in full sight of the grandfather's hut.

"Why! It's like you said!" Jamy cried in delight. Then she hugged Heidi in her excitement. But Heidi herself had seen the grandfather and broken away.

"Grandfather! Grandfather!" she called out. "I'm home! Your Heidi's home!"

He turned from the bench beside the door where he was sitting, rubbed his arm across his face as if to make sure a mist was not forming before his eyes. First he recognized his friend, the doctor. Then he saw Heidi and his face broke into smiles, while tears of joy rolled down his wrinkled cheeks. She ran to him and hugged him hard before she introduced her friend from school.

"How do you like my surprise?" asked the doctor, shaking his hand. "Heidi and Jamy are here for a month. I know Heidi will want to be with you at first, but later today they plan to go up to the high pastures."

"Ah! That is fine!" said the grandfather. "Come, Peter, milk my goats and we will have a bite to eat."

Heidi was already seated on the bench, her head

pressed lovingly against his shoulder.

"Did you know," the grandfather asked, stroking her soft hair, "did you know that the greatest joy of my life is the Tuesday when Peter brings your letter to me? How happy I am to see you! Tell me, are you still planning to come back to Dörfli and teach when you have finished school? Is it true that you want to stay here with me?"

"Of course, Grandfather," smiled Heidi. "I want to live in Dörfli for the rest of my life!"

Jamy gave her a queer look, as much as to say, "You'll change your mind," but Heidi was too happy to notice. Only Peter saw it and read even more from it than Jamy had meant.

The doctor stayed on with the grandfather to keep him company when Jamy and Heidi started off with Peter up to the pasture. Before long they reached the place where Peter usually stopped for the goats to rest and graze. It was a little green plateau jutting out from the mountainside and commanding a view of the whole valley. Here Peter spent long hours, gazing out and whistling from time to time while his animals munched the sweet grass.

He carefully stowed his lunch away in a little dugout he had made so the wind would not blow it away and invited the girls to place their lunches there, too. Then he stretched himself out on the grass to enjoy the air and sunshine.

The sky was a deep blue. All around rose the high mountain peaks, shining with snow and ice, while far below, the deep valley still lay in the shadows of early morning. Heidi and Jamy, sitting together on the high plateau, felt the wind blow sharp and cool in their faces. Above their heads, birds circled in the blue air.

Meckerli, Peter's new pet, came close to rub his head against the girls, making little friendly bleats; then he danced over to Peter and rubbed up against his shoulder. One by one, the other goats came over to make friends. Each had his own manner of greeting. Jamy was enchanted.

Barli, the darker one of the grandfather's two goats, examined each person separately with an anxious air; then she stood perfectly still and stared until she was told, "Yes, yes, Barli, that's fine. You may go back and browse."

Peter recited the names of all the goats, and Jamy seemed surprised that he could keep them all in his head. These difficult names seemed harder to her than a history lesson at school.

While they were being named, the goats capered about, full of mischief. Schwanli and Distelfinck (Thistlefinch), who was thin and slender of build, would charge both together at Peter and bowl him over if he was not stretched flat on the ground. Donnerkeil (Thunderbolt), the mother of Meckerli, was very proud. She came within two feet of the strangers and raised her head to look them over with the air of someone who disdains familiarities, afterward walking away with great dignity. The Turk, who was the oldest billy goat and thus felt his importance, butted all the other goats out of his way and then stood bleating grandly to show that he was chief over the herd and meant to keep the others in order. But Meckerli refused to be pushed about. When the big goat came near him he would run to Peter for protection. There he felt perfectly safe, although if he met the old Turk alone he trembled from head to foot.

And so the sunny morning passed. Peter pulled out his lunch and stood quietly leaning on his stick, eating and thinking, while the girls unpacked the lunch the grandfather had fixed for them.

After lunch Peter decided he would like to try a new way to the higher slopes, for that afternoon he planned to take his little troop farther up the mountain. He finally decided on the left path because on that side was a meadow with little bushes the goats particularly loved. The path was steep, especially near the top, and there were some dangerous places along the edge of the cliff. But Peter knew the way well and he hoped the goats, remembering the good meal which awaited them at the top, would follow closely and not stray off.

He led the way up the rocks and the girls followed, while the goats climbed the difficult places with ease, one after another. Little Meckerli stayed close to Peter.

From time to time the goatherd would catch him by the neck and pull him up over the steep rocks. At last they all reached the grazing place safely and the goats began to nibble eagerly at their favorite plants and bushes.

Jamy almost held her breath as she stood there on the top of what seemed to be the whole world. She could not have imagined a more beautiful spot. The air was filled with the scent of the Alpine flowers which grew everywhere—vanilla orchids, fringed gentians, little blue harebells, primroses, and jonquils. And she picked a whole armful of golden rockroses.

"They'll wither before you've reached home with them," Heidi told her, "but, if you like, Grandfather will dry them for you."

She watched her as she picked still more flowers, until her apron was full, remembering with what pleasure she had picked her first flowers on this same mountain, even though the flowers did wither and their splendid colors fade.

"Easy, easy there," said Peter to the goats. "Be quiet and don't butt one another. In a minute one of you will be at the bottom of a ravine with his legs broken. Distelfinck, where do you think you're going?" he cried, glancing up the rocks.

The lithe little animal called Distelfinck had climbed out onto a steep rock ledge. Perched there above a sheer drop, she stood looking back at Peter as much as to say, "See how daring I am! See how close I can go to the edge of the rock!" Another step and she would be over! Peter scrambled after her as quickly as he could; in a few seconds he reached the jutting rock, seized the imprudent Distelfinck by one leg, and dragged her back. Heidi was close behind him, remembering how it was this goat that had always given him trouble. Between them, they led her down to join the others, but Peter held onto her until he was quite sure that her mind was on her grazing again and not on further escapades.

"But where is Meckerli?" cried Jamy. Donnerkeil, the little kid's mother, was standing all alone, staring down over the edge of the cliff. Jamy had noticed that when the kid was not with Peter, he always followed closely beside his mother.

"What have you done with your baby, Donnerkeil?" asked Heidi, running up to her in alarm.

Donnerkeil acted very strangely. She wasn't grazing, just standing perfectly still, her ears pricked forward as if listening.

Peter looked down. He heard a feeble, sad little bleat below—a tiny, piping voice calling for help.

"Don't cry, little Meckerli, I'm coming," he called as if speaking to a child.

Stretching full length on his stomach, he peered over the edge. Far below him something moved. Then he saw his little pet dangling from a branch growing out of a crevice in the rock. He was crying pitifully. The branch had stopped his fall. Even now, if the branch gave way, he would fall and break his little bones.

Trembling with anxiety, Peter called down, "Hold on, Meckerli! Stick to your branch. We are coming to get you."

But how could they reach him? Peter saw immediately that it was hopeless to attempt to climb down from where he was. The ledge of rock was clean-cut and offered no possible footing. But Heidi pointed to the rock below. "The Rainy Day Rock," she called it, because she and Peter had often found shelter there during a storm. Peter might be able to reach Meckerli if he climbed up from there.

It was a good suggestion and Peter was already heading down the path.

"Jamy, look after the goats. We are going to rescue Meckerli," cried Heidi, running after him.

Heidi had seen how fond Peter had become of the little goat and so she prayed as she ran, "Dear God, please help Peter save his little Meckerli."

Fearlessly the boy climbed the rocks without once looking down, until he neared the branch. There he planted his two bare feet solidly against the Rainy Day Rock and, reaching up, managed to grasp the trembling, frightened animal and hand him down to Heidi, who was just below him.

Once they were back in the meadow Peter was

overjoyed, and Heidi breathed another prayer, this time of thankfulness, as they both sat down on the ground to caress and calm the frightened little kid.

It was now nearly time to go home, so they went back to the plateau and found Jamy anxiously guarding the rest of the flock. She felt quite pleased with herself that none of the goats had strayed.

At the sound of Peter's horn, all the goats started to move. Peter carried Meckerli on his shoulders. He was so happy that he sang his favorite song from beginning to end. This delighted Jamy and she declared he would be asked to sing it over and over until she knew it by heart.

Heidi had an errand to do for the grandfather in the village and so she and Jamy went with Peter all the way down to Dörfli. Here Peter brought his goats to a halt beside the village fountain and once more blew on his horn. At once, children came running from all directions to sort out their own family goats from the rest. Women appeared from the neighboring houses; one took her goat by the horns and another by the cord about its neck, and in no time at all the little herd had disappeared. Peter left the girls then, and went home singing. Heidi did her errand and she and Jamy trudged back up the mountain to the grandfather's hut, but they were talking and laughing and praising Peter all the way.

8

GRANDFATHER!" begged Heidi when they were sitting around the table after supper that evening. "Won't you tell Jamy some of your wonderful stories? I have promised her that by the time she returns to school she will know almost as many old legends as I do."

"These legends are long," the grandfather said, "and you have had a hard day in the pastures. I save my stories for rainy days. But," he added, much pleased, "I believe it will rain tomorrow."

The Alm-Uncle was rarely wrong in prophesying the weather. The next morning, though the sky was clear, Peter left very early carrying a raincoat over his arm, and the girls did not go with him. Around noon, heavy clouds rolled overhead and the storm broke. Peter found shelter for himself and his goats under the

Rainy Day Rock, as usual. To his surprise, another goatherd was there, but without his goats. It was Gerard from Ragatz. The two boys stood still for a moment, then greeted each other with a hearty "Hello!"

"I didn't know you came all the way up here with your goats," the other boy said to Peter.

"Sometimes," Peter replied, "but not every day. Usually I stop in the first meadow or round about there. Why did you come up here?"

"I wanted to see you. I have to pick up two goats from you to take to Ragatz where they have been sold."

"Are they your goats?" asked Peter.

"Surely, they belong to us. I don't keep goats for anyone else. I am no longer a goatherd," announced Gerard rather proudly.

This surprised Peter. As Gerard once had been elected goatherd, Peter could not conceive of him not continuing the job. But instead he spoke as if being a herdsman was an unworthy occupation, something to be ashamed of. This troubled Peter and he began to wonder if Heidi's school friend Jamy might not have the same idea.

While the two boys were talking, the clouds lifted again and the sun came out. Peter decided it would be a good time to eat his lunch. He invited Gerard to share it with him. Talking as they went, they reached the dugout where he had stowed it away and Peter brought out his sack filled with bread and ham and cheese. With a flat stone for a table, they sat down to eat with good appetites.

After they had eaten all there was in the sack and drunk two bowls of fresh goat's milk, Gerard stretched back, leaning on his elbows. Peter sat still, looking off into the depths of the valley.

"But what do you do at Ragatz if you are no longer a goatherd?" he asked. "One must do something."

"Of course I do something, and do it very well," retorted Gerard. "I sell eggs. Every day I take my eggs around to as many inns as I can. I sell them to the hotels, too."

Peter tossed his head in disdain.

"And what is that? I would not want to sell eggs. I would a thousand times rather be a goatherd. It is a much better thing to do."

"How do you make that out?" asked Gerard.

"Eggs aren't alive. They don't follow you around all day like the goats do. They aren't glad to see you when you come to get them in the morning. They don't rub up against you and understand everything you say to them," said Peter. "You can't possibly love your eggs the way I love my goats."

"And you, what do you get out of it?" interrupted Gerard. "Only a few coins a week at the most. And you had to jump up at least six times while we were eating, simply for that little good-for-nothing kid you are so afraid might fall. Is that fun?"

"Of course," said Peter promptly. "I do it willingly, don't I, Meckerli? Your little legs are so unsteady and you are still very small." And again he led his pet away from the edge of the cliff where he was always straying. When he came back and sat down, Gerard observed, "There's another way to keep the goats from falling down on the rocks without always running after them."

"What way is that?" asked Peter.

"Plant a stick in the ground and tie the goat by the leg. She'll carry on badly, it's true, but she won't get away!"

"Don't you think for a minute that I'd ever do that with this little kid!" said Peter indignantly and, pulling Meckerli toward him, held him tightly in his arms as though he would protect him always from such cruel treatment.

"Well, you won't be bothered with that one much longer," continued Gerard. "He has only a few more days to come up here."

"What! How do you know that?" Peter demanded with a start.

"Bah! Don't *you* know?" Gerard mocked him. "The schoolmaster doesn't want to raise him. He's not strong and will never make a solid goat that's worth his keep. So the hotelkeeper at Maienfeld told me to bring him over next week."

Peter turned pale. At first he couldn't utter a word,

but then he exploded with grief, "No! No! They wouldn't dare! No, Meckerli, they wouldn't dare to do that. I wouldn't let them. No! That is impossible!"

"Look here!" Gerard said, facing him about suddenly. "If the kid means that much to you maybe I can get my father to buy him. But you'll have to do something for me first."

And Gerard held out something in one hand which he half-covered with the other. It was something that sparkled between his fingers where the sun shone on it.

"What is it?" asked Peter.

"Guess!" he said.

"A ring?" hazarded Peter.

"No, but something like it. I found it on the path down to Maienfeld."

"Oh, then it doesn't belong to you," concluded Peter.

"Why not? I didn't take it from anyone. I almost stepped on it yesterday when I came up from peddling the eggs. I could easily have broken it. Since I didn't, I guess I can keep it," Gerard reasoned.

"But someone has lost it, and you should put up a notice," Peter insisted.

"No, no, I won't do that," cried Gerard, alarmed that Peter should take this attitude. "Look! Look at it! It is solid gold. The shopkeeper in the village will be glad to buy it if you will take it there and sell it for me. We can split the money and no one will ever know."

"I won't do it," said Peter quickly. "And you're forgetting that the dear Lord in heaven hears and judges everything you say."

Gerard raised his eyes to the sky. "As far as that?" he said doubtfully. But, nevertheless, he started to speak in a lower tone.

"He can hear you anyway," said Peter with assurance.

This made the ignorant boy uneasy. He regretted having told Peter anything about his find. But it was now too late to do anything about that. He would have to think of another way out of the difficulty.

"Peter," he said suddenly, "I will ask my father to buy Meckerli anyway, if you will promise not to say a word about this. Then the schoolmaster cannot have him killed."

Gerard had opened his hand and Peter had seen the thick gold cross lying in his palm. He knew it was valuable and that certainly someone would claim it. Inwardly, he was having a difficult conflict. He knew that if he said nothing it would be as though *he* were keeping something which did not belong to him. But, on the other hand, there was his tender little Meckerli who would be unmercifully sacrificed to the butcher! And he could prevent that by keeping silence.

The kid came over and lay down at Peter's side, looking trustfully into his face as though he were sure that the boy would always protect him. Peter couldn't let the little thing die! A goat's life was worth more than a cross of gold or the coins Gerard promised him if he sold it. And he was buying Meckerli's right to live only with silence.

"All right. I accept," announced Peter dully.

"Good, put it there!" And Gerard held out his hand for Peter to take and seal the pact. He seemed quite content with the bargain. As Peter apparently had nothing more to say and he had a long road before him, Gerard decided to go on with the two goats. So he said good-bye. When he was gone, Peter called his troop together and also started down the mountain, but he was lost in thought and not once did he whistle or sing.

A Struggle Within

9

THE NEXT MORNING Peter passed silently and discon-
solately through the village. He called out the goats
and went on his way up the mountain without singing
a note, without one joyful yodel. He trudged along, his
head hanging as if he were afraid, and from time to
time he turned around as though someone might be
following to question him.

Peter himself could not understand his own misery.
He was rejoiced to have saved Meckerli's life; he wanted
to sing as he always did, but the song stuck in his
throat. The sky was heavy, too, and Peter decided that
it was because of the dismal day that he felt so sad. He
now persuaded himself that when the sun shone again
he would be gay once more.

No sooner had he reached the meadow than it started

to pour. He sought refuge under the Rainy Day Rock and watched the rain fall in torrents; lightning flashed across the sky and the thunder rolled. The goats came up, too, and stood close under the rocks to the right and left. Distelfinck, always so delicate, wanted to protect her beautiful shining coat and came to sit under the rocky arch in front of Peter. From her comfortable corner, she looked out peacefully at the rain. Meckerli stood close by his protector under the rock. Rubbing his head tenderly against Peter's knees, he looked up at him as though surprised because, for the first time, Peter was silent, paying no attention to him. Barli, too, scratched the earth with her little hooves and bleated as much as to say, "All morning you have not said a single word to us."

Deep in his thoughts, Peter stood leaning on his stick. He always carried a stick, something like a shepherd's crook, but he needed it especially when it rained to keep himself from slipping where the path was steep. Poor Peter had lots of time to think things over as he stood for hours under the rock. He turned over in his mind the promise he had made Gerard, and the more he thought about it, the more he was convinced that, since the other boy was keeping something which did not belong to him, he himself was guilty because he had sold his silence. He had done something which was not right and so even God would be against him. He was overcome with remorse, and he thought if Meckerli were to fall over the cliff again, God would not help him as He had done before. He and the little goat would fall down the precipice and be dashed to pieces as a punishment.

"No! No! That must not happen!" he exclaimed aloud, for his thoughts had formed a very clear picture before his eyes.

"I will tell," he resolved at last. But then he saw the butcher's knife hanging over little Meckerli's head, and that picture was just as clear as the other.

So the torrent increased and the weight on his conscience grew and grew. Thus the whole day passed. In the evening he returned as silent as when he left. Heidi and Jamy were waiting for him and ran out to the stable.

"Peter, what is the matter?" they asked. "Why don't you sing anymore?"

He turned around grimly. "I can't," he answered, and went on his way as fast as he could without looking back.

"It is very strange that he doesn't sing or whistle anymore. Something has certainly happened to him," said Jamy.

"It's this awful rain that puts him in a bad humor," decided Heidi. "Or else he is vexed because you are here and he doesn't have me to himself anymore. He felt that way about Clara once, when she was crippled, and became so angry he pushed her rolling chair over the edge of the mountain. But he was a little boy then, and he was truly sorry. I thought he had outgrown such fits of bad temper."

"He is only a goat boy," said Jamy.

Heidi's eyes flamed.

"He is *Peter!*" she said. "And even if he does have fits of temper, I wouldn't change him. I wouldn't change him any more than I'd change Grandfather," she added. "They're both part of my life here in Dörfli . . . and I love them!"

Jamy looked at her in surprise. Could she realize what she was saying? What spirit! And what wonderful loyalty to her own people!

The next day was as gloomy as the day before. The sky was overcast. Peter went about with the same heavy weight on his conscience. He sat down under the same rock and his thoughts turned around in the same circle. No sooner had he decided to tell everything he knew about the cross than he saw the butcher's knife on little Meckerli's throat, and he began all over again.

When evening came he was so exhausted with thinking and thinking and nothing resolved that he walked along sadly and slowly in the steady downpour. The schoolmaster, standing in his doorway, called out to him sharply.

"Come along more quickly with those animals! They are already wet enough. Why do you walk along like a tortoise? The villagers will want a new goat boy soon if you cannot be trusted."

The words stung. A new goat boy? And in the stable at the grandfather's, where he had returned Schwanli and Barli, Jamy had stopped him to ask, "Peter, are you going to be a goatherd all your life?"

On the following day the sky cleared and the sun shone brightly. It seemed to Peter that God was looking straight down at him from the blue depths of heaven. The advice of his blind grandmother came back to him clearly. Long ago, when he had first gone up to the pasture, she had drawn him aside and said in her gentle and yet certain voice, "Remember, Peter, up there on the Alm you are very near to heaven. God will see and hear everything you do and say. You cannot hide anything from Him. But also, He is nearer to you and can help you. Since you are too far away to call anyone else if something should happen, call on Him. He will hear you and surely come."

So, at last, it became very clear to Peter what he must do.

"Forgive me, Meckerli," he cried over and over as he helped the little goat down from the pasture. "Dear God! I must be sure that I am doing right, but please, please don't let Meckerli die!"

When Peter stopped at the grandfather's, the old man looked up and asked with deep concern, "What is it now, unhappy goat general? Heidi has been telling me that you have lost your voice."

"I have something to confess," said Peter, hanging his head.

"Out with it then," the old man prompted him.

"Something was found," replied Peter with great difficulty.

"Something found!" Jamy started up from the table where they had just sat down to supper. "I lost something, too—my beautiful gold cross!"

"Yes, that's what it was," said Peter.

"What are you saying? Was it a thick gold cross on a velvet ribbon?" asked Jamy excitedly.

"Yes, it was," said Peter in the same indifferent tone.

"But have you got it? Where is it? Give it to me! Where did you find it?" spluttered Jamy.

"It wasn't I who found it," Peter said. "It was Gerard of Ragatz."

Jamy wanted to know all about it and suggested sending someone for Gerard right away.

"I will be glad to go myself," said Peter. "In fact, I think I should go. If he still has it, I will bring it back."

"If he still has it! But why wouldn't he have it?" exclaimed Jamy. "What would he do with it? Where and how did he find it and how did you know about it?"

But Peter kept his eyes on the floor and was afraid to tell. Before he left, however, Heidi took him aside and he told her the whole story.

"Dearest Peter!" she said when he had finished.

"And so the grandmother still helps us! If it had not been for what the grandmother told you, you might have kept this secret, mightn't you, Peter?"

"Yes," he confessed, "I might. But now Meckerli will be killed."

Heidi smiled. "Didn't you ever think of buying him yourself, Peter? Didn't you ever think of owning your goats instead of just keeping them for other people? Nearly every man in Dörfli owns his goats."

Peter pondered this a moment, and left for Gerard's in a thoughtful mood. Jamy had promised Gerard an even larger reward than he would have received if Peter had sold the cross and they had split the money between them. He was angry at first when he heard that Peter had told, but the reward soon pacified him and he surrendered the cross. It was too late for Peter to climb back up the mountain with it that night, and so he took it home with him to keep until the following morning. Before he went to bed he carefully counted out what money he had. It wasn't half enough to buy the kid. The schoolmaster was stern and would sell him for no less than he would receive from the hotel-keeper. In the future, however, Peter resolved to save and buy his own goats, as Heidi had suggested. But that would be too late to save Meckerli!

The next morning, very early, Peter arrived with his band of goats and silently handed Jamy her treasured cross. Then he went on up to the pasture.

When he returned in the afternoon, Jamy ran to meet him.

"Why are you still so sad, Peter?" she asked.

He shook his head. "I am thinking of my little goat. How much longer will he be alive, my little Meckerli?" and his face wore such a woebegone expression that Jamy was touched and decided to keep her surprise a secret no longer.

"Do you know how happy you have made me, Peter?" she asked. "Without you, Gerard would never have returned the cross. So now I want to make you happy, too. Today, while you were up in the pasture, Heidi and I went together to see the schoolmaster. I wanted to give you a reward and the nicest reward I could think of was little Meckerli. Pick him out of the flock now, Peter, and take him home. He belongs to you!"

For a moment Peter was so surprised he could only stare at Jamy. Then he found his voice and thanked her a thousand times, and Heidi, too. For Heidi confessed the idea had been hers.

As he swung down the path with his goats, Peter started to sing and never before had he sung so gladly. His voice rang out across the valley, bursting with joy. The sun shone brightly in the blue sky. The grass was fresher and greener than ever after the three days of rain, and all the flowers bloomed in their brightest colors. It seemed to Peter that never before had the mountain, the valley, the whole world been so lovely. He felt that he couldn't hold all the happiness in his heart.

It was still early when Peter and his troop arrived in the village. Brigitte heard him shouting to her before he was in the house.

"He belongs to me! Meckerli is mine!"

He stopped first at the stable where he fixed a soft bed for his pet. Then he went into the kitchen, and as he ate with an excellent appetite he told his mother of everything that had happened. Brigitte listened patiently to the long story and when he had finished she said, "Peterli, all your life long, remember these last few hours. Be guided by your conscience. You would have done so this time if you had thought of the people who trust you before you thought of the little goat."

Before he went to bed, Peter went out to the stable once more to make sure Meckerli was still there. He could not yet believe such good fortune had befallen him at last and that the little white kid was really and truly his.

10

THE TALL, somber pine trees did not sway and sing in the wind as usual, but were motionless in the still air. The mountain, too, was strangely patched with amethyst light and black shadows, while, above, the glacier shone blue and cold in the sun.

This morning Peter loitered anxiously around the hut with his goats.

"Heidi! Jamy!" he called, and the two heads immediately appeared in the small window of Heidi's little loft room.

"Good morning, Peter!" they greeted him. "Don't shout so! We aren't coming up on the mountain with you today. We're going down to the village."

"Please!" Peter begged. "I've been waiting for you to come. The goats are extra mischievous today and I'm afraid something may happen. You seem to calm them, Heidi."

But the girls only laughed and teased him and finally threw everything they could find out of the window
at him—blankets, a sheet, hairbrushes, an apron, and
even a shoe. Indignant at such treatment, Peter walked
off whistling to show his indifference.

Heidi and Jamy were busy about the house and the
morning was almost gone before they noticed the heavy
sultriness creeping up from the valley and closing
down from the sky at the same time. After lunch, the
grandfather gave them errands to do in the village.
"First, tell the doctor all is well here, and give Brigitte
these two cheeses. One is for Peter. Pass by Bert-
hold's and ask if my *hotte* is ready, and then stop at
the baker's and get two pounds of salt. You've fed so
much to the goats there is none left."

As he spoke, the old man's eyes wandered over the
mountains and then down the valley where everything seemed to be smothered under a thick veil of
fog.

"It is going to storm today. The mountain looks
bad!" he murmured. He had always been able to in-
terpret weather signs which seemed to escape everyone
else. "If it breaks early, stay overnight in the village.
The doctor will be happy to have you."

"But, Grandfather," protested Heidi, "you will be
alone here with the goats if we stay in Dörfli."

"Don't be anxious, my child. The dear Lord will look
after us," replied the kindly old man.

He stood watching the two girls as they ran gaily down the path. When they had reached the bottom of the big hill they turned and waved and he waved back. And not until they were two small specks entering the village did he turn back to stroll around the little house. Everything was spotless and in perfect order. He stopped a while to look at the pine trees, which he loved the more because of Heidi's music.

"But why do they seem so different today?" he pondered. "What makes them so remote?"

The mountain shone in a weird violet light. Toward the close of the afternoon the blue transparency of the glacier became frankly black. Suddenly the pines began to rustle as though in warning. They shook from the ground up to the topmost branches, and yet there was not the slightest trace of wind. In the west, far off over the valley, the sky was black. Even the sunlight looked dull, as though seen through a thick gloss.

The grandfather's anxiety, however, was not for himself but for Heidi, down in the village. "The storm will surely break before night," he thought. "If only the doctor will think to keep the girls with him!"

Peter came down from the pasture earlier than usual and called, "Uncle! Come here and look! See how the sun is fading out."

"Good day, goat general!" he smiled in answer. "Are you back already?"

"The goats are restless. Schwanli started down first

and all the others followed her. I couldn't make them go back again. They act afraid."

"They feel the storm in the air," the Alm-Uncle told him. "Hurry down to the village and tell your mother that Heidi and Jamy are to stay with her tonight."

"But, Uncle, you will be alone with the goats!" objected Peter.

"I'm used to it," he replied impatiently. "Go quickly now, and do as I tell you."

Peter, who had never quite overcome his boyish awe of the old man on the mountain, turned and ran, followed by the frightened goats.

In the village Heidi and Jamy finished their errands and then went to call on the pastor who had been such a good friend to Heidi when she was a child. At four thirty, when they arrived at the big house, the doctor was waiting for them in the doorway.

"Come in quickly, girls," he called. "Tea is waiting. Brigitte has made a mountain of little cakes so high that you will need someone to help you eat them!"

"They won't last long! Here comes Peter. Now all we shall have to do is sit and watch them disappear."

"Peterli, watch how many you take," his mother chided him as they all sat down to do honor to her cookies.

The doctor, watching Heidi's happy face, remarked,

"This mountain air has certainly brought back all your excellent color and also a very excellent appetite. You are not sorry I took you away from your music, are you, Heidi?"

"Sorry! Dear Doctor, of course not. I am happier here than anywhere else in the world." And she rested her head a moment against his shoulder, looking up into his eyes to convince him of her complete happiness.

After tea Brigitte packed a basket with the little cakes that were left and handed it to Heidi. "For your grandfather," she said.

"We'll hurry home with it," Heidi began, but Peter stopped her.

"You're not going up on the Alm tonight," he said. "The grandfather says so. He says there's a storm brewing and you're to stay here with us."

"A storm!" exclaimed Jamy. "But the sky is blue! You must be dreaming!"

"The sky *was* blue when you came in," said Peter, standing at the door and pointing, "but look! While we've been talking and eating cakes, it has changed to black!"

"I'm going up on the mountain all the same," announced Heidi. "I am not afraid of the storm, and I don't want Grandfather to be alone tonight."

"But he sent that message," insisted Peter. "He said to tell the doctor—"

"Thank you, Peter. We will obey the grandfather,

won't we, Heidi? And without discussion, because we know he is right," said her godfather.

"But . . ." started Heidi.

The doctor only looked at her, surprised, and she lowered her eyes in confusion.

Toward evening everything grew black, as though Dörfli had become a village of shadows. It seemed as though the houses were shut down under a lid and the air was so heavy it was hard to breathe. In the west lightning flashed from time to time, but there was no sound of thunder. Uneasy, the neighbors in the village went about their houses and stables seeing that everything was closed up tight. Very often when there was a fire caused by lightning, the poor animals perished in the flames because they could not escape, but the custom persisted. Always, the villagers of Dörfli locked their stables against the storm.

In the big house, Heidi and Jamy were preparing to go to bed early because they planned to start up the mountain with Peter at the first cock's crow. But first they listened to Brigitte as she repeated all the gossip of the village. More than one family was bitter against the schoolmaster.

"I'm only thankful Peterli is out of school," she said with a sigh. "The goats can bring no harm to him."

"Is the school so bad then?" Jamy asked. "Can they not hire a new teacher?"

"That is not so easy," the doctor put in. "The children run wild. No teacher can manage them."

"I could," said Heidi quietly.

But they all laughed to think of their little Heidi managing an intractable school. So she said no more of it, although the conversation had left her deeply impressed.

The doctor had asked Heidi to bring her violin when she next came to the village as he had not heard her play since her return from school.

"I shall play very badly," she demurred, "because I have been so long out of practice."

"We shall be an indulgent audience," the doctor told her.

She raised her bow and began. But it was not one of the pieces she had learned at school that she played. It was the wild, sweet song she and Peter had learned together. The music of the pine trees sounded through it. The shrill notes whistled and moaned.

"The storm has got into the violin," she said, laying the instrument down. "Listen! It's already beginning to break."

On the mountain the wind roared through the pines and larch trees; then the houses in the village creaked and shook. The first crash of thunder sounded through the valley like a rolling of drums, gradually dying away, to be followed by another and another. For half an hour, crash after crash continued. Heidi and Jamy clung to the doctor, watching at one window while Peter and Brigitte peered anxiously from another. Suddenly someone ran through the streets crying, "Fire! Fire on the mountain!"

Heidi turned pale and rushed to the door, followed by the doctor and Jamy. Brigitte hurried after the girls, carrying the capes which they had forgotten. It had begun to rain, and the thunder now seemed farther away. High on the mountain a bright glare shone out. There was no possible doubt in Heidi's mind. It was the grandfather's hut!

Several men joined the doctor, who was already climbing in all haste up the Alm, his emergency case ready.

"There's nothing we can do," said one of the men. "It's too late."

"We may still be in time," another told him. "Go ahead, Doctor. I will follow with a jug of coffee for the uncle if—" He stopped short, but everyone understood.

For an instant Heidi stood perfectly still, as though turned to stone; then she broke into a run, crying all the way up the path, "Grandfather! Grandfather!"

She ran on and on, ahead of all the others, strangled by sobs but with dry eyes. Over and over she repeated, "Grandfather! Oh, Grandfather!" Paying no heed to the path, she stumbled against the rocks, tripped and fell a dozen times in her haste, pausing for nothing, seeing nothing but the blazing fire high above.

Someone caught up to her and cried above the noise of the rain, "Heidi! I saw a tall shadow pass before the flame. It's your grandfather, I am sure!" And Peter, almost breathless from running, stopped while Heidi shook him by the arm.

"Is it true, what you say? You saw a shadow before the fire?"

"Yes, Heidi," the boy managed to reply, "I did, and my eyes are very keen. . . ."

Heidi, dragging him by the arm, kept on her way up the path, but more slowly now because she, too, was breathing hard.

"Peter! Did you hear something?" she demanded.

"No," he answered, "nothing but thunder and the rain."

In a moment little running feet sounded before them and two shapes appeared and stopped short in their path.

"The goats!" they cried in the same breath.

They hurried on and soon came close enough to the hut to see the bright flames and the sparks going high into the air. Fear clutched at Heidi's heart.

"Peter! Where's Grandfather?"

"I saw him pass in front of the flames," the boy insisted. "Let's look higher."

At last they found him under the pines. He was sad and weak. He gazed at the ruins of his home where he had lived for so many years, where Heidi had come to him, bringing all the joy of the world in her little-girl hands! All was gone and he felt stripped of everything that was near and dear to him.

"God has taken my nest. I hope he will soon take me, too," he was thinking sadly. He did not see Heidi until she threw herself into his arms.

"My poor child!" he said.

For a moment Heidi could only sob, torn between the joy of finding him alive and sadness for the sorrow she saw in his eyes. Finally, in a broken voice, he murmured, "I should have gone, too."

Peter drew himself up to his full height before the stricken old man and, somehow, his boyish fear of the Alm-Uncle melted into sympathy for the grandfather whose spirit he must lift up for Heidi.

"I will help you rebuild your hut," he announced, "and next year we will all sing together:

> "High on the mountain is a new chalet!
>   For Jean so brave and true
>   Has built it all anew. . . ."

The grandfather smiled.

At that moment a crowd of people arrived from the village. But the doctor was first.

"The damage is not so great, my good friend, since you are not hurt," he said joyfully. "Come down at once to the village and tomorrow we will lay plans for a new house, larger and more comfortable. How about giving Heidi a whole room to herself instead of the bed in the loft that she has always had?"

"Heidi will like that," the grandfather said, and was quite cheered.

The End of Vacation

11

THE NEXT DAY the grandfather and the doctor went up on the Alm with Peter and his goats. They stopped to see what remained of the hut, and before another sun had set they had laid plans to rebuild. A few days later, Peter and the grandfather and two helpers from the village were at work on a new house.

When the house was completed, even the grandfather felt no regrets for the hut that had gone up in flames. There was nothing of the lonely hermit's hut about the fine, new house that took its place. There was a bedroom for the grandfather, an even larger room for Heidi, a large comfortable kitchen, and a living room which could be used as a bedroom when Clara and her father came to visit, as they always did toward the end of summer.

The grandfather had carried a great many things out of the hut when he discovered it was too late to save it. The chair he had made long ago for Heidi, her little bed, the big copper kettle he used for cheese-making over the fire, the table, and many other things he had made in his shop behind the kitchen. Now he had a workshop which was entirely separate and more convenient. Schwanli and Barli also had a separate stable. But, best of all, the new house was built on the same ground as the old hut and the same pines whispered and sang above it. When Heidi looked out of her window she saw the same view as always—the Falknis with its snowy peak and, below it, the whole village of Dörfli.

"We do not need to come down to Dörfli now," the grandfather remarked, looking thoughtfully over the valley. "Dörfli is growing up to us."

And so it seemed. Cottages were being built higher and higher up the mountainside. Heidi and the grandfather were no longer without neighbors, although the new house was still far above the others—like an eagle perched on the edge of a rock.

"But, Grandfather," Heidi protested, "you don't mean you are going to stay up here the year around, just as you used to?"

"Why shouldn't I? When you have finished school, you will be with me."

Heidi thought of the winter, of the glorious snows, of the long sleigh rides down the mountain. On her skis, too, she could skim over the surface of the snow and be in the village in no time. But always there would be the hard climb back again.

"The doctor will be lonely," she said.

"He has Peter and Brigitte."

"They won't always be with him. Peter plans to re-build his mother's house as soon as he can and, if I teach, how can I ever climb this mountain from the school?"

"We shall see," was all the old man would say.

But Heidi knew he wanted nothing more than to be in this house with her to care for him as long as he lived.

They had been in the house three days and every-thing was in order, the grandfather comfortable in his room and Heidi and Jamy snugly settled in theirs. The living room, or what would be the living room, was still bare. But the grandfather was busy in his shop carv-ing out new furniture which seemed to Jamy quite the most splendid hand carving she had ever seen. Heidi thought so, too. She was watching him fit the two ends of a finely carved settee onto a frame which was to be roped to make it more soft when suddenly Jamy ran to the door and pointed.

"Heidi! Heidi! Someone is coming up the moun-tain. They've passed the last house in the village and so they must be coming here!"

"It's Herr Sesemann—and Clara!" Heidi cried out in delight. "Oh, now you shall meet Clara! It was because of Clara that I went to the school at Rosiaz."

"And it was because of you that Clara walks, I have heard," Jamy replied quietly. "See how fast they are climbing!"

"I'll put on a kettle for tea and we shall have a fete out under the pines," Heidi decided.

After she had greeted her friends from Frankfurt, she ran down to leave word for Peter, for no fete would be complete without him. He and Brigitte and the doctor trudged up the mountain in time for the spread. Brigitte, luckily, had made some fresh cookies and these she brought along and with them a fine piece of sausage from the doctor's larder.

Under the pines there was a soft carpet of needles and on these the table was placed with the grandfather's bench on one side and three of his chairs on the other.

"I have never seen such a spread!" exclaimed Clara when it was ready. "All we need now is Sebastian to serve it—"

"And Fräulein Rottenmeier to spoil it," put in Heidi with a giggle.

During the whole meal they talked gaily of the year Heidi had spent in Frankfurt, recalling the organ-grinder and the kittens and all the other incidents which had upset poor Fräulein's peace of mind, until Jamy confessed to an actual homesickness for Mops, the school cat.

"I had hoped you would go on with the violin and

study in Paris with me," Clara said wistfully afterward when they were talking over Heidi's plans to return to Dörfli to teach.

"I can play for the people up here," Heidi said, "and I should be homesick in Paris. Grandfather has been alone quite long enough. Don't urge me, Clara, for my mind is quite made up. I shall always stay here and you shall always come to visit. I am happy here and I shall stay as long as I live."

"Very well, Heidi," Clara said resignedly. She knew Heidi well enough to be sure she would not change her mind.

The August evenings were beautiful. During the whole week Clara stayed she never once missed watching the sun go down. Heidi and Jamy went up on the high rocks with her and usually Peter came along. Often the doctor and Herr Sesemann came, too, to listen, while Heidi played her violin and the young people all sang to the enchanting music. They seemed to fill the whole valley with their music. Even the sun went down as though keeping time to the notes Heidi played on her violin. Always it disappeared far too quickly behind the rose-colored mountains. As its last rays glowed on the peaks, they would stand so that, to the grandfather in the house below, they looked like shadows against a background of rose-colored flame.

In the evenings they all gathered in the large kitchen

of the new house and listened to the grandfather's wonderful tales.

"Just one more story," Clara always begged when it was time to go to bed, and the old man would begin once more.

So the summer passed. Jamy found the grandfather's stories far more interesting and entertaining than anything she learned later from her school books. By the end of her vacation she knew the history of Switzerland, with its many beautiful legends and Alpine songs, almost as well as Heidi or Peter. And Clara left, resolving once more that nothing should ever prevent her from coming for at least a week every summer to the mountains where she had once found health and strength and the courage to walk again.

With September, Heidi and Jamy returned to school. The trees were hung with yellow leaves. Lessons began and Mademoiselle Larbey planned several autumn walks. One afternoon the pupils went to visit the chateau of Chillon, where Bonivard was imprisoned for six years, and they saw the path worn in the stone floor by the feet of the condemned man chained in his small cell. Heidi wrote to her grandfather about it and was shocked and hurt beyond words when he wrote back that there were many cells like it. In Dörfli, he said, the prison was much the same.

Heidi had always known there was a prison in Dörfli, but she had thought of it before as necessary and right.

Now it seemed unmerciful and cruel. She wondered what sort of people were kept there.

"When I go home to Dörfli," she announced to her schoolmates, "I am going to do something about the prison. People aren't meant to be caged up like animals in the zoo. It isn't right."

"What are you going to do?" they laughed. "Go and play music for the prisoners?"

"I might," she retorted. "Why mightn't I?"

They joked about it and called her a little crusader.

"She's going to cheer up the prisoners!"

"And teach the girls in Dörfli how to sew and knit. . . ."

"And the boys how to read."

"And marry the little goat boy," Eileen finished sarcastically.

"Is it such an awful life?" Jamy said wistfully. "I'd gladly change mine for it."

Even Eileen, who had looked down on Heidi, became a little envious as she listened to more and more tales of the summer at Dörfli. And when Heidi left for home, at the end of school, the good wishes of all her schoolmates went with her.

A Broken Flowerpot

12

ONE SUMMER EVENING, as the peaks of the Falknis were illuminated by the last rays of the sun, Heidi sat at the window of her room in the grandfather's house, looking out across the valley. Her heart was filled with longing and yet she wanted nothing more than to stay right where she was so that every evening she could watch the splendor of the mountains, and every night the music of the pines and larch trees could lull her to sleep. She loved the grandfather and was happy with him. How, then, could she be lonely?

Her thoughts were very far away when suddenly she saw Peter walking up the path with a letter in his hand. It bore an official stamp and, when Heidi opened it, she found it was an answer to her application to teach the village school.

"Perhaps this is what I've been waiting for," she said, her eyes lighting up. "It will give me something to do."

"You have not been idle here with the grandfather," Peter reminded her.

"I know, but I've always wanted to teach."

"So that's what you've always wanted!" Peter said abruptly and left her, still holding her letter.

Neighbors in the village had advised her against making the application. The school was a disgrace, they said. Nobody could manage the unruly children, least of all an inexperienced girl like Heidi. But Heidi remembered that Peter, too, had been unruly as a boy. Yet she had taught him to read. If she could do that much then, surely she could do more now. She felt certain that if the children in the school were loved and understood, they would respond, in turn, with love and understanding.

The schoolhouse where Heidi was to teach was built on a shoulder of the whitecapped Falknis. She came early on the first day and stood by the window looking out on the green pastures and pine trees and rolling slopes and, beyond, the rocky pinnacles. She followed the twists and turns of the little road up the Alm until it came to an end at the grandfather's house. The green grass growing on either side of the footpath was neither tall nor tufted as in the valley, but short, tender, sweet pasturage, dotted with little Alpine flowers in brilliant colors.

She loved this view from her window. A pot of sweet-smelling mignonette bloomed on her windowsill. She had brought it down from the house on the Alm and the grandfather had planted it. She could see him moving about now, a little black speck on the green slope. It was good to be so near him when, if she had gone to Paris to study the violin as Monsieur Rochat and Clara Sesemann had both wanted her to, she would be so far away. She could see Thoni, the new little goatherd, on the mountain, too. Peter was no longer there. He had a fine flock of his own goats now and kept them, for the present, in the doctor's stable.

The new goat boy, Heidi thought, should be in school. She glanced at the schoolhouse clock and found it was already late. But her classroom was empty. Silence was everywhere except for the ticking of the clock. Outside, not a child was in sight with the exception of Thoni, minding his goats. Nine o'clock passed, and then ten o'clock. Noon went by without one child, boy or girl, putting in an appearance. The afternoon was just the same.

"Perhaps this is a holiday and I don't know it," Heidi thought. Gathering her things together, she was about to leave the school when a tumult of voices sounded outside. Going to her window, she saw an army of children heading down the path toward the school, crying at the top of their lungs, "Let me see it! Let me see it! If you didn't steal it, what are you hiding it for?"

"I'll tell the shopkeeper on you!" One voice rang out louder than the others. "He'll put you in prison—and that's worse than the dungeon."

The boy who was running ahead turned around and Heidi, watching from her window, could see a look of wild terror in his eyes. It was terror such as the prisoners of Chillon must have felt and, in her thoughts, Heidi could again see the footmarks worn on the stone floor. Throwing open the window, she called out, "Stop!" at the top of her voice.

"Look out, Chel!" one of the children cried. "There's the teacher at her window looking out at you! Just wait until you get in school! She'll put you in the dungeon!"

What dungeon were they talking about now? Heidi wondered. Determined to find out, she again called out to the children. Chel raised his head, saw her, ducked again, and a moment later someone in the group had picked up a stone and sent it flying toward the window. Heidi drew back just in time. Instead of striking her, it struck her flowerpot, sending pieces of pottery flying in all directions. The beautiful mignonette fell to the floor, broken. The whole group of children stopped stock-still and stared, then scattered like frightened rabbits and the school was as quiet as it had been before.

Walking sadly over to the window, Heidi picked up the pieces of her flowerpot. What could cause children to act like that? Had the old schoolmaster frightened them out of their reason? Or was it the dungeon? Heidi looked about her. The schoolroom was the same as she remembered it, except for the scratched desk tops and the broken blackboard. A heating stove was in the center, then the six rows of desks, three on either side of the stove. She remembered how, on cold days, the children used to huddle next to the heat. The room had been a comforting place then. The schoolmistress had been kind. But with the schoolmaster came a reign of terror and Heidi could easily understand the change. Punishment had been his first thought whenever anything went wrong. But could he have been cruel enough to put children in a dungeon and, if so, where was it? The schoolhouse had but one room and two coat closets at either side of the teacher's desk, one for the girls and one for the boys. Heidi opened the door to one of these and found that all the hooks had been removed and that the one little window had boards nailed across it.

"This must be the dungeon!" she exclaimed and closed the door quickly. No wonder the children were afraid to come to school.

The next day the schoolroom was deserted, and the following day, also. Heidi was no longer surprised, but something had to be done about it. She waited until the morning of the fourth day and then walked over to the house on the big rocks where she knew the school warden lived.

Just before she reached his house, she suddenly found herself face to face with little curly-haired Germaine Grube whom she knew should have been in school. The child stopped short in surprise. Her hands flew to her head as she attempted to cover her tangled mop of hair.

"Are you the new teacher?" she gasped. "You mustn't see me. Mama said so. I'm not fit to come to school and meet a lady teacher."

And the poor child began to cry bitterly as though, even now, she might be punished for her ragged appearance.

"There's Mama now," she sobbed at length, pointing to a woman coming along the path toward the house with a shovel over one shoulder and carrying a basket of dead wood over her arm. Two young children hung onto her skirt, and another little girl ran alongside, catching hold of her mother from time to time so as not to be left behind.

The woman would have passed by, but Heidi stepped out into the road quickly and spoke directly to her.

"Frau Grube, I am the new teacher and I have come to find out why the children do not go to school."

"We hear there was a fight," the woman said, leaning on her shovel. "I want the girls to wait until the beating is over. I do not wish them to see it."

"But there will be no beating," Heidi exclaimed. "I have no intention of punishing the child who broke my flowerpot. I'm sure it was an accident and had best be forgotten."

"But if you do find out," Germaine ventured, peer-

.ing from behind her mother's skirts, "you'll put Chel in the dungeon and we'll have to hear him scream."

"I won't put Chel or anyone else in the dungeon," Heidi said firmly. "We won't be using the dungeon this year. I intend to have it made back into a coatroom."

There was a momentary silence. Then Germaine's mother again began speaking. "Even so, I cannot send the children to school. When one has to work from morning until night, it is impossible to spend the time to dress them properly. A lady teacher will expect them to be combed and washed and have all their clothes mended. The schoolmaster forced them to go. Otherwise I would not have sent them looking the way they do!"

"I hope I shall not need to force them," Heidi said gently. "Please send them tomorrow. I will see that they are washed and combed at the school."

"You are very kind," the woman murmured.

Heidi bade her good evening and walked on to the warden's house. She found him sitting on the doorstep enjoying his pipe while his wife prepared his dinner.

"I came to ask you what I must do," Heidi began. "The children are not coming to school. They seem frightened to death of being locked in the dungeon. Did you know, Warden, that the old schoolmaster had fitted out a prison in the school cloakroom?"

"Yes," he replied calmly. "I knew it. I always leave

the teachers to their own methods of punishment."

"But that is horrible!" Heidi cried. "The old school-master was cruel. It was his nature to be cruel, for he was even cruel to his goats. I believe children can be governed better by kindness."

The warden laughed dryly. "Get them to come to school and maybe they can. Shall I send an officer after them?"

"Thank you, no," Heidi replied. "We must not frighten them any more than they have been frightened. I think they will come by themselves."

Disheartened, she walked home to the doctor's house where she always stopped for her midday meal. Around the table, she talked over her difficulties with Peter and Brigitte and the doctor. It grieved them all that Heidi was not happy with her school as she had hoped to be.

"You should have taken my advice," the doctor said, "and kept up your studies with the violin."

"You were doing very well with your drawings, too," Brigitte put in.

"But Monsieur Rochat told me I'd never make a musician and I'm sure I could never be an artist. What do you want me to be?" Heidi asked suddenly, turning to Peter.

"I don't like schoolteachers," he replied, and that was all the answer he would give.

"But, Peter, I taught you once," she insisted. "And

children must be taught."

"Try it a little longer," Brigitte said kindly. "The villagers are discouraged now and the children are frightened because of the old schoolmaster. And don't listen to Peterli. The oxen put him in a bad temper."

"So it's the oxen, is it?"

"They're harder to manage than the goats," confessed Peter.

Nevertheless, as Peter drove his new oxcart down to Maienfeld where he marketed the milk from his fine flock of goats, Heidi felt her heart swell with pride. What better thing could a boy do than keep his own oxen and milk his own goats and sell the milk to be made into fine cheeses? Gerard, with his egg business, could no longer scoff at Peter, for his herd had been started with the schoolmaster's one weak little goat which Gerard had thought only fit for the butcher. Later, when the schoolmaster left Dörfli, Peter bought his whole flock with the coins he had managed to save.

But Peter was unhappy in the village. The doctor's big house seemed to shut in from all sides and often he, too, was filled with longing. To go back on the mountain was his one great ambition. He was saving coins again, but when he spoke to his mother about the new house he planned to build on the Alm, she said, "But why, Peterli? The doctor is glad to have us here."

"We can't look out," he said, "and the street is noisy and the goats are away all day in the pasture while I must drive the stupid oxen to town. I tell you, it's like being clamped down under a cover! I'm going up to the uncle's. He knows what it is to have freedom, and up there I can breathe."

The Alm-Uncle was firm in his determination not to come down to the village for the winter. Heidi was uneasy about him until she heard of Peter's frequent visits.

"He says to tell you he has God and the goats and the pine trees for company," Peter told her, "and that you are not to worry. He is not alone."

But she knew he was only thinking of her good when, in his heart, he longed for companionship. During the first few days of school, she often wondered why she had decided to teach at all.

Chel

13

WHEN HEIDI CAME to school the morning after she had seen the warden, she found a group of little girls waiting for her. They came into the schoolroom slowly, each one trying to hide behind the others. Finally one asked, "You're not going to beat the boy who broke the flowerpot, are you?"

Heidi shook her head, smiling slowly.

"And you're not going to put him in the dungeon?"

"There isn't any dungeon in the school," Heidi said. "It's a cloakroom now. As soon as we have a window in it again, you can have it for your wraps."

The girls seemed pleased at this. But still they stood around, twisting their fingers, as if there were something more they wanted to say. Finally Germaine explained. "They want to be combed and washed. I told them you said you'd comb their hair and they want it in a braid like yours."

Heidi laughed out loud from sheer relief.

"I am delighted," she said at length. "You can't think I'm such a fearful person if you want your hair fixed like mine. How many of you know how to make a braid?"

By the looks of their tousled heads, none of them knew how to make a braid very well. They all said they wanted to learn.

"That will be our first lesson then. I want you all to form in line with the largest girl first so that you make steps down to the smallest."

Pushing a little and laughing a great deal, the girls rushed to do as they were told. When they were all in line they followed Heidi to the fountain where, one by one, she washed their hands, their arms, and their heads. Then she stood them in the sun to dry their hair while she went to her desk to get a comb. Dividing each girl's hair into three strands, she made exactly twelve glossy braids.

"There!" she said, looking over her glowing accomplishment. "Now you know how to braid your own hair."

Her labor was well spent. The children looked from one to the other, laughing and happy, and each one appeared transformed.

"Now," said Heidi when they were again standing in line, "I am going to tell you a little secret. We can't have any regular lessons until the boys come back to school so we will put the books aside and learn something new. How many of you know how to knit and sew? Raise your hands."

Not one hand went up.

"Very well," concluded Heidi, "each one of you bring a torn dress with you tomorrow, or a stocking, or vest, or a little shirt, and we will begin to sew. Those of you who are good, who do what I say and try to learn quickly, will receive a comb as a reward. Now you may go and spend the day as you please."

The little girls ran off down the path, looking from one to another as if they could hardly believe such kindness had been shown to them. After the schoolmaster's harsh discipline, it was, indeed, a change. Word spread rapidly that the new teacher was gentle and kind and was teaching the girls exactly the sort of things that industrious girls needed to know. But it had been a boy who broke the flowerpot and so each boy, fearing he would be blamed, waited for the other to come to school first.

For eight days now the sewing and knitting lessons had been going on. The promise of new combs worked like a charm. Each little girl was eager for her reward. Several of them, indeed, had already received it. The class had the wholehearted approval of all the mothers, and each day new pupils arrived. Heidi had given such a large order for combs to the village shopkeeper that he suspected her of starting a little business on the side, and when he received still another request for thread, needles, skeins of wool, tape and yarn and string, he was convinced of it.

Heidi, busy with her needle, was patching a torn vest here, darning a stocking there, when suddenly a terrible racket sounded in front of the school. She ran to the window and saw a group of boys yelling and shouting names. In the middle of this fracas two men were trying to drag away a boy who struggled furiously, biting, kicking, scratching, and fighting with such energy that the two men, even with the help of all the screaming boys, were unable to move him. Finally, overcome by numbers, he let out a despairing cry which went straight to Heidi's heart. Pushing her way through the crowd, she faced the men who were struggling with the boy. She recognized him as Chel, the one who had caused the other fracas when her pot of mignonette had been broken.

"What has he done?" she demanded. "Where are you trying to take him?"

"What has he done?" cried one man. "What *hasn't* he done, you'd better say! This time he even attacked the warden, who ordered him to be punished. We're bringing him to the school dungeon."

"No! No! Not the dungeon!" screamed the child. "I tell you, I never did it. I wouldn't hurt Distelfinck for the world."

"Distelfinck!" exclaimed Heidi, more puzzled than

ever. "What has the warden's goat to do with all this?"

"Chel wounded her," the man explained. "He threw stones at her and broke her leg so she can't walk. And when the warden scolded him for it, he threw stones at him, too. He should be punished well for that!"

"Perhaps," said Heidi. "But he certainly should not be put in a dungeon. Why, that room in the school has no air or light with the window boarded up the way it is. I wouldn't put a beast there, much less a child."

"But I didn't do it," the boy insisted.

"Well, what did happen to the goat then?" one of the men demanded, turning on him angrily. "Her leg's broken, all right. She can't walk! She just lies on the straw trembling, and the veterinary can't be reached until tomorrow."

"Poor Distelfinck!" murmured Chel, who seemed to have forgotten himself, thinking of the little goat.

"Why don't you explain what did happen, Chel?" Heidi asked gently.

The boy shook his head sadly and made no reply.

"This is what happened," the first man said. "The goat disappeared from the pasture. Later that evening she returned to her stable, limping and half-dead. Her broken leg was bound up with a tie which the boys recognized at once as belonging to Chel. He had wrapped up her leg, thinking that no one would notice it."

"No, that is wrong," interrupted Chel. "I did it so

she could get back to the stable without her leg hurting too much."

"You hear? He admits having touched the goat!" exclaimed the second man.

"You knew, then, that the goat had a broken leg?" Heidi asked Chel, whom she instinctively believed in-·nocent. "How did it happen if a stone did not hit her?"

"She fell off the rock," replied Chel sadly.

Heidi could easily believe that, remembering the many narrow escapes the goat had had when Peter was the village goatherd.

"If she fell off the rock, how did she climb up again?" asked one of the onlookers. "And how could you tie up her leg at the bottom of the rocks?"

"I climbed down to her and helped her up," said Chel.

"You hear what he says now?" the man addressed the crowd. "You weren't even near the goat in the meadow or the goatherd would have seen you."

"He is incapable of telling the truth," said the man who was holding him. "Come along, boy, into the schoolhouse dungeon—"

"No! No!" cried Heidi. "I won't allow it!"

Chel started to fight again as the man attempted to drag him. "I didn't do anything!" he screamed, turning to Heidi.

"He threw a stone at the teacher's window, too, and broke her flowerpot!" cried one of the children.

A new expression of terror spread over Chel's face and he turned his eyes away from Heidi as much as to say, "Now it's all over!"

"That has nothing to do with this affair," said Heidi quickly. "No one knows whether he is really to blame for the goat's being wounded or not, and he should not be punished until we are sure he is guilty. In the meantime, why don't you leave him with me? I will take him to Dr. Reboux who, I am sure, will gladly be responsible for him."

The men agreed to this, apparently relieved to have the youngster off their hands. Heidi's sewing class was upset for the day, so she dismissed the girls and took Chel directly to the doctor's house. He walked the whole distance in silence but, at the door, he suddenly tried to jerk away. But the doctor appeared in time and Heidi announced gaily, "Here is the prodigal son, Doctor. Have you killed the fatted calf? This boy has been pretty badly frightened," she added more seriously, "and he would probably appreciate a soft bed for the night after he has stowed away a little bread and cheese. Do you think you could manage it?"

"I'll try. Come, son. Nobody is going to hurt you," the good man assured him. "What is all this trouble you've been having? Let's talk it over and get the story straight."

Chel glanced up at the doctor with his half-frightened, half-savage brown eyes and then turned away as though to avoid looking him in the face as he repeated the same confused story he had told outside the school.

"You understand, Chel, that I want to help you?" the doctor asked when he had finished.

"Yes," said Chel, "but I don't know why."

"Because," the doctor replied, "I was once a boy just your size and I know how it feels to be accused of something you haven't done. I know also how it feels to have done something wrong and be scared to death that somebody will find out. So, you see, you can speak to me frankly, as though I were your father. Did you tell the truth?"

Chel seemed more and more surprised, as though he could hardly understand the doctor's words. He was silent, looking long and questioningly into his face.

"Tell me, Chel. Don't be afraid," he urged.

Then, as though he were coming out of a dream, he breathed deeply and said in a clear voice, "Yes, I told the truth. I didn't throw a stone at Distelfinck. She was the most beautiful goat in the neighborhood and I wouldn't hurt her for anything."

"I believe you," the doctor said. "But I still don't understand. They say that the goatherd would have seen you if you had gone to the pasture where the goats were grazing."

"That is not where I was. Distelfinck did not fall from that side," protested Chel.

"I still don't understand. The goat was with the

herd. Where could she have fallen then?"

The boy made no reply.

"Did you see her fall?" asked Heidi.

"No, I heard her bleating down there on the rocks," he answered painfully, trying to avoid Heidi's eyes.

"And you, where were you then?" the doctor asked.

Again the boy was silent.

"Listen, Chel," Heidi said, taking him by the hand. "It's for your own good that the doctor is asking you these questions. If he can explain to the warden who is so angry with you, then you will not be punished. And if you have done something wrong and are truly sorry, he will see that you are not punished, either. And, in any case, you won't be put in the dungeon. Nobody will be put in the dungeon while I teach the school."

"You wouldn't say that if you knew what I did," murmured Chel, his eyes on the floor. "I threw a stone at you and broke your flowerpot."

"But you're sorry for that, aren't you?" asked Heidi gently.

Chel nodded, without raising his eyes.

"All right! Give me your hand and look at me. You see, I am not angry. Since you are sorry, I forgive you and we won't think about it anymore. It's wiped out and forgotten."

A warm light shone in Chel's eyes as he looked back at Heidi.

"Do you still not want to tell the doctor what happened, where you were, and where the goat fell, so he can explain to the others?"

He lowered his eyes again and only shook his head.

"We'll let it rest for now," the doctor said kindly. "He may feel differently about it after he's had some food."

He called Brigitte and asked her to set an extra plate on the table. But when the good woman saw it was Chel who was to stay, she looked at him with distrust. She had heard terrible tales about him and knew that his father was known as the terror of the countryside.

When Peter came in and heard that Distelfinck had been wounded, it was hard to convince him of Chel's innocence.

"Why do you take this boy's part?" he demanded of Heidi. "If he's innocent, why won't he tell the whole story?"

"It may be hard for him to talk," replied Heidi. "You ought to understand that, Peter. Words never came to you very quickly, either. This boy is very much like you might have been if you hadn't had your good mother and the blind grandmother to teach you what was right—"

"And you, Heidi," he put in. "Remember when you taught me not to beat the goats, though I still carried the hazel rods to torment you?" he added. "I hardly ever needed to use them."

"This boy doesn't need to be taught to be kind to

goats. He already knows that," Heidi said, "or he would never have bandaged Distelfinck's leg so carefully. He only needs to be taught to be kind to human beings—and that's hard when they have been so cruel to him. But the doctor can teach him if anyone can. Don't you think so?"

"I think so," Peter replied. And, at last, he seemed satisfied that Chel should stay.

14

EARLY THE NEXT MORNING when the doctor went into his room, Chel was so absorbed by a little painting which hung on the wall that he didn't hear his footsteps. The doctor went over to him and he jumped and turned around as if he had been caught doing something which was forbidden.

"You may look at the painting as much as you wish," said the doctor graciously. "How do you like it?"

"Yes, the white is beautiful! Those flowers are all white! I don't know what they are."

The doctor studied his face a moment. Beneath his savage expression, there seemed to be almost a spiritual look, as though the boy had been surprised while kneeling at the altar in a church.

"I can see you appreciate beauty," the doctor said.

"Have you ever tried to draw or paint?"

Without replying, Chel glanced fearfully behind him.

"Is the teacher gone?" he finally asked in a whisper.

"Yes. Today is Saturday and she has gone up to her grandfather's on the mountain."

"And Peter? Peter thinks I'm guilty. I could tell."

"Nothing of the kind," replied the doctor. "Peter is only young and restless and feels like a fish out of water in my big house when he is used to being with his goats up in the pasture."

"I know how he feels," said Chel, and then closed his lips tightly as though he had almost told something he wished to keep to himself.

"Besides," the doctor added, "Peter was very fond of Distelfinck."

"I was fond of her, too," said the boy sadly as he turned his face toward the window.

Brigitte fixed a nice breakfast for the ragged little stranger but he ate with a poor appetite.

"Drink your milk," she said, pushing his cup toward him.

"I am not thirsty for goat's milk," he replied. "I will just have the cheese."

After breakfast Chel went back to his room and the doctor gave him a book.

"I have a call to make," he said, "and you must stay here until I return. You are not to leave this house until the warden has an explanation of the accident to his goat. That is what I promised so, you see, this house is really your prison."

"I like it here," said Chel, looking about him as though this prison pleased him very well.

"Then promise me you will stay here quietly until I come back. You may read while you are waiting."

"I can't read," said Chel simply, sitting down with the book.

After he had made his call, the doctor decided it might be well to have a talk with the warden himself before questioning the boy any further. Here was more of a problem than appeared at first. It was a question not only of who wounded the goat but of who wounded the boy's spirit and what could be done to help him.

When the doctor found the warden he was in his stable kneeling on the straw beside Distelfinck. He was muttering something to himself and the doctor could see that he was very angry.

"How is the goat?" he asked. "Has the veterinary come?"

"He came all right, and this thing is going to cost me money! Come here and look at this." He motioned the doctor. "Distelfinck just lies there on the straw, like you see her. The poor goat is in pain, too. And while she is there, she doesn't give any milk. She knew better than any of the other goats where to find the most delicious grass and her milk was marvelous—never very much of it. The others gave more than she, but milk! Ah! Milk like the honey from flowers! And now look what the brute has done to her!"

"Do you mean Chel?" asked the doctor. "It is about Chel that I came to see you. I am convinced, Warden, that the boy didn't purposely harm your goat. He loves her and he is hurt because she is in pain. One thing is certain. The goat fell somewhere and Chel never stoned her!"

"You think so?" cried the warden, becoming more and more angry as the doctor defended Chel. "The whole valley knows the doings of that boy. He lies and steals and throws stones! There's not one household that does not stand in terror of him!"

"He has behaved himself very well in my house," the doctor replied quietly.

"He has behaved himself, has he?" sneered the warden. "Why, that boy doesn't know how to behave himself! Probably learned a thing or two from his father, who was killed on one of his night prowls. Nobody knows where he hangs out. And just try and get him to work! One look at those baby soft hands of his and you can tell he'd never do a tap of work."

The warden's resentment against Chel loosened his tongue. He had never been so eloquent. The doctor listened to all his complaints with a sad heart, for he had become genuinely fond of Chel and wanted to set him right. Besides, he could see that Heidi trusted the boy and she was seldom wrong about such things. Chel didn't say much, it was true, but his character seemed to be quite different from what the warden and the villagers seemed to think.

In any case, the doctor was sure of one thing. Chel had not purposely harmed the warden's goat. He felt this too strongly to doubt his intuition.

"Whatever else he may have done, this time you are accusing the boy unjustly," he said firmly. "I see no reason to keep him a prisoner in my house any longer and so I intend to give him his liberty and hope that he will return to school."

But the warden wouldn't listen to this. Heidi, he said, would never be able to manage the boy.

"I knew this business of having a lady teacher wouldn't work," he went on. "I told the school board but they were set on making a change. Well, they've got it. Sewing lessons! And not a boy that will come to school. Another week of this and I'll send an officer after the boys in spite of everything Heidi says. Kindness may work with the girls but the boys need to be handled by a man."

"Let me handle this boy in my own way then," the doctor said.

"Very well, handle him! I wash my hands of the whole affair," the warden retorted.

He turned his back and walked into the house.

When the doctor returned, he found Chel poring

over the book he had given him. With a movement quick as lightning, he hid something in his pocket. The doctor had a terrible suspicion which he regretted a moment later. Chel *could not* be hiding something he had stolen from him! He seemed so genuinely glad to see him.

"Chel, you are no longer a prisoner here," announced the doctor. "I told the warden I believed you had not purposely harmed his goat."

"Were they able to fix her leg so she won't limp?" asked Chel anxiously.

"Yes, the veterinary came," he replied, a little surprised to see Chel more concerned about the goat than he was about himself. "You may go whenever you wish, but come back as often as you like in the evening and we will talk. Come to school, too," he added as an afterthought.

Chel's face clouded with apprehension at this invitation.

"Do I have to go to school?"

"Eventually," said the doctor, "you will have to go to school. So you may as well begin. And another thing," he continued, "look for work, no matter what. In Maienfeld at the big farms you will surely find something to do. Everybody should work. And, also, eat regularly where you are supposed to and don't stay away nights and make people suspicious of you. No one knows where you go. If I talk to you like this, Chel, it is only because I want very much to see you on the right track, and then whenever something happens everyone won't say immediately, 'Chel did it!' "

All the joy went out of the boy's face. He held out his hand to the doctor, raised troubled eyes to his, and was gone.

15

THROUGHOUT THE VILLAGE of Dörfli admiration for Heidi grew stronger every day. Mothers and grand-mothers opened their eyes in surprise when they saw the splendid work the children were doing in school. Boys, as well as girls, were learning new things every day. For the boys returned and regular classes began as soon as word spread around that Chel had confessed to throwing the stone that broke Heidi's flowerpot.

One day when she came into the classroom, Heidi saw a large pot of flowers standing outside on the windowsill. When she opened the casement, a delicate perfume arose from a clump of white Alpine violets growing in a beautiful earthen pot. She was delighted. But who had put them there?

She thought first of Chel, but where could Chel find such a lovely pot of flowers? And besides, if he was so anxious to please her, why hadn't he done as the doctor asked, and come to school? Nothing had been seen of him for weeks. He had never returned to visit the doctor and the poor man was nearly heartbroken, blaming himself for sending the boy away without finding out, for certain, with whom he lived and what he intended to do.

From time to time Heidi asked the children at school and villagers she met on the street if they knew what had become of Chel. But not one of them had seen him. He had not once come to the village for his meals and nobody had any idea at all where he slept. She did learn this much, that when his father died six of the villagers had kindly offered him bed and board and that he had spent a little time with all six, coming back occasionally for meals. But he had not been back for a long time now. Nobody knew what had happened to him and there were a great many who did not seem to care.

Heidi became more and more worried. At night, as she knelt at her window and looked out across the mountains, the dear Lord seemed very near and she often prayed to Him, asking Him to keep Chel safe and return him to those who loved him.

One evening, long after the grandfather had gone to bed, Heidi stood before her window looking out at the stars and seeing how the moonlight made a white halo over the peak of the Falknis.

But tonight there was something fearful about the

147

moonlight. It had none of the friendly warmth that the
sun threw over the mountain peaks all day, nor the
rosy glow it reflected on them in the early evening. It
made ghosts of the glaciers and black shadows of the
crags between. Heidi shivered and was about to pull
in the shutters when suddenly she heard quick steps
outside and then a rap at the door. She went down
quickly and asked who was there.

"Let me in!" a voice cried. "I have news!"

Heidi threw open the door.

"Peter! It's you! What do you want at this hour?"
she asked in sudden dread. "Is your mother all right?
Has anything happened to the doctor?"

"Nothing has happened to anyone," Peter replied
placidly. "But I found out where the boy goes and
thought you'd like to come along and see."

"You found out about Chel? Well, tell me, Peter!
Don't stand there like a goat."

"I can't tell you," Peter said, "but if you will come
with me, I will show you where he goes."

"Show me?" cried Heidi, growing frightened. "Do
you want me to come now?"

"Yes, you can come now if you'd rather. It's full
moonlight and I can easily find the way."

"No, Peter, I can't go out like this in the middle of
the night," Heidi protested. "Only tell me, is he safe?"

"He was never safer," replied Peter, smiling.

"Then wait until morning and I will come with you.

Sleep here. The grandfather has room. And tomorrow, when it is daylight, I will go wherever you take me, and you can show me whatever you want to show me. Now, good night, Peter." And she ran back upstairs to her own room, leaving Peter on the new bed her grandfather had carved out of white logs.

The sun had barely risen when Peter opened the door and called. But Heidi was already up and dressed for the journey.

"Come, let's go," she said. "I hope you remember where you promised to take me."

"Yes, I remember very well," he said. "I was over the path only yesterday. Shall we go now?"

"Drink this cup of milk first, and eat a piece of bread. I will eat something, too. We cannot start without breakfast. Who knows where we may find ourselves!" she added, smiling.

"Who knows?" said Peter, and smiled back.

The grandfather had arisen and made his guest comfortable the night before and now he bid Peter a hearty good morning.

"We're going to church in the mountains this morning," the boy told him. "You will not miss us, Uncle. You will have the goats and the pines and the church bells in the village to keep you company. And when we return you may have still another guest to eat cheese with you."

They started off in gay spirits. Rosy clouds hung in

149

the sky. Before long the sun would be fully up. Pine trees along the road stood dark against the sunrise, and each tree had a different shape. Peter had chosen the path that led to the top of the pass. They climbed silently together up the mountain. The sun rose and everything around them sparkled and glistened: the flowers along the path, the larch trees poised on the peaks, the ledges of rock over their heads. Everything shone in its best Sunday dress. Heidi's eyes were shining, too. But where was Peter taking her?

They had been climbing for over an hour and by now should be almost at the top of the pass. Peter left the road abruptly and turned left, on the side of the steep slope covered by trees. They came to the edge of a wood which looked impenetrable. The huge old pine trees grew close together; here and there fallen trunks and dead branches lay tangled on the ground. Still Peter pushed on. He jumped like a squirrel over the dead boughs and the crumbling tree trunks.

Heidi stopped short.

"No, Peter, we cannot get across here," she declared. "You must have forgotten the way."

"No, no, I haven't forgotten," he insisted. "See how I have marked the trees!"

She saw a fresh cut in the bark and knew he was not mistaken.

"Come, Heidi. You can follow me," he urged, holding out his hand to help her.

She hesitated an instant, but finally took his hand and climbed safely over. He pulled her along after him through the branches and the brush; crawling over the old, decayed trunks, trampling the deadwood underfoot, but always keeping a sharp eye for the markers he had made to show him the way. Holding down tangled branches and vines, he patiently set aside all obstacles so that Heidi might follow. At last they came out into a clearing, leaving the forest behind them.

Never had Heidi seen anything more beautiful than the scene which lay before her eyes. She found herself in a sunny meadow full of flowers—red primroses, anemones tinted with rose, sweet-smelling violets, and gentians of a deep, deep blue. Tall peaks covered with snow towered before her into the blue sky. Between the ridges glistened immense glaciers which looked as though they were slipping toward the valley like large rivers frozen in their course. The flowers glowed with color and brilliance against their background of sparkling ice and snow.

"Peter! Peter! Remember the grandmother—her hymn . . . her garden!"

Overcome with joy, Heidi was hardly able to speak. Everything seemed to float before her eyes in the enchanted morning light. She ran to the edge of the meadow and, as she had expected, looked out upon the whole valley as far as Maienfeld. But how jagged the rocks were! They bristled like spears at the foot of the precipice. She was leaning over the edge to see how deep it was when she felt herself pulled by the skirt.

"Heidi! Take care! That is where Distelfinck fell," cried Peter, still clutching her skirt.

"Distelfinck? But how did you know? Who told you about it?"

"Chel," he replied simply.

"Peter! You've made friends with him! I should have known it. He is so much like you."

"You could have made friends with him, too," Peter said, "if you hadn't been a teacher. But come, we're nearly there!"

"Nearly *where?*" asked Heidi. "Peter, where are you taking me?"

"You wanted to see what happened to Chel," he replied.

A sudden fear overtook her. "Was it Chel's father who showed him this road? They say in the village that he was a smuggler. Was it over these rocks that he carried his smuggled goods down to the valley?"

"Over there, no one can go down," said Peter, pointing to the ledge. "Chel's father never took him over this road. He found it by himself. Heidi, you must not believe what the people in the village say."

"I know they are filled with prejudices," she replied. "They are suspicious of everything which they do not understand. It is because I want the children to grow up with more understanding than their parents that I am so anxious to teach. Tell me, Peter, why did you say I could have made friends with Chel if I hadn't been a teacher?"

"Because he's afraid of you," Peter replied. "He wanted to come to school when he found out how kind you were. He did come one day. But he saw that the boards were still across the little window. So he knew the dungeon was still there and he was afraid because, so often, he doesn't know what is right and what is wrong until he finds himself being punished."

"I see." Heidi's reply was slow. Peter's words had set her thinking. "I must do something about that window," she said. "I shall see the warden about it tomorrow."

A Talent Is Discovered

16

As THEY WALKED together along the narrow ledge of rock, Heidi held fast to Peter with one hand while, with the other, she caught hold of the dwarfed trees that thrust out from the crevices. Finally they reached a mass of rock which jutted out like a roof and underneath it was a platform where, at last, they could walk more securely.

Heidi looked down at the abyss beneath her, shivered, and then, turning her head, found she was standing before a deep cave.

"Peter, what's this—" she began. But a voice cried at her wildly, "You can't come here! It's mine, I tell you! It's mine! I won't let you in!"

It was Chel and he was stooping over to pick up a rock when Peter seized him firmly by the arm.

"Wait a minute, boy!" he said quietly. "Is that any

way to welcome a guest? I intended to show your teacher where I found you, but now that you are here, you can show her yourself."

The boy's eyes were as savage as a little animal's.

"I'll show her!" he cried. "I'll not have my things taken away!"

"She won't take your things away, Chel."

"She's a teacher!"

"Yes," Peter replied, making a queer grimace at her, "she's a teacher. But, to me, she's the same little girl who used to come up to the pasture and, if I know her, she'll be as pleased as I was when you show her your secret."

"But I found this place," the boy whimpered. "It's mine, where nobody can follow me."

"Why should you be afraid of being followed?" asked Heidi. "Up here, you can have nothing to hide."

Peter laughed at this, and the boy looked at him.

"Show her what you have to hide, Chel. That's what I brought her here to see."

Chel looked up at Heidi, but she was smiling at him kindly.

"You won't take everything away from me like the schoolmaster did, and not let me go on?" he asked, half-yielding.

"I would never take away anything that belonged to you, Chel. Peter will tell you I wouldn't do that."

"Will you let us in, then?" asked Peter.

The boy hesitated, looked up at their faces, then stepped aside quietly and let them pass.

Sunlight penetrated for a little distance into the cave, but beyond all was black. In the entrance stood a roughly made table and a bench. Four stakes firmly planted into an uneven board formed the table, and the bench had been made the same way. The table, the bench, and the ground around them were covered with broken pieces of pottery of all imaginable colors. Heidi had to bend down her head to go in. At Peter's invitation, she sat down on the little bench and looked around. Before her were several pieces of paper covered with paintings and now she understood why the place was littered with broken crockery. The pieces had been used to mix color on—strange colors that Heidi had never seen before. She examined the drawings.

"What is this? Who made it?" she asked.

"I did," replied Chel, as though confessing a fault.

"But it's lovely!" she exclaimed, fascinated by what she saw on the paper. It was a painting of white roses and lilies over a tomb, ivy of a surprising yellow-green wound around the flowers and the stone. Heidi studied it a moment, wondering where she had seen it before. Then she recognized it as being a copy of a picture that hung on the wall in the doctor's house in Dörfli. The drawing was beautiful and the copy exact, in spite of the strange colors.

"Did you paint all this, Chel? These roses, these lilies,

this ivy, too?" she asked in amazement.

Chel nodded, his eyes to the ground.

"You aren't going to take everything away from me and not let me paint anymore?" he asked anxiously. "Peter said you wouldn't. You're not annoyed with me?"

"My dear boy! Annoyed with you? Why, I am delighted! How pleased the doctor will be when he hears of this wonderful talent!"

"But I thought it was wrong," Chel faltered. "The schoolmaster said it was wrong to draw. He—he took my drawing away from me and put me in the dungeon."

"You see?" put in Peter.

"I see," Heidi replied. "The poor, stupid schoolmaster—not to recognize such talent! You were probably drawing when you had been asked to do something else, Chel. That is the reason. But in my school there is a new art class and, if you will come, I shall give you good colors and you will see how different your flowers will be! But tell me first, Chel, do you stay in this cave all the time? Do you stay here at night?"

Suddenly a change came over the boy's face. He threw back his head and the hunted expression disappeared from his eyes.

"You are not angry!" he cried. "And you will give me good colors! And my flowers will be beautiful! I want to tell you everything, everything I know. But where shall I begin?"

"Tell her what you did and where you went when you were away for days at a time and no one knew anything about you," prompted Peter.

"I went off," he said, raising truthful eyes toward hers. "My father was no longer there and I don't remember my mother at all. I went with the other boys and we quarreled and threw stones at each other. Whenever I hit one of them, he would cry right away, 'I'll tell my father on you!' Then his father would come and beat me. But when they hit me with stones, I had no father to run to. So, in the end, I went farther and farther away, so that no one would find me. The farther away I went, the more beautiful the flowers were. I wanted to pick them all. I did pick big bunches but in the evening they withered and all the colors faded away. I thought, 'If only I could copy them, then I could keep them for always.' So I drew the flowers with pencils I took from school. I took paper, too. But the schoolmaster didn't keep colors so I tried very hard to make them. Without color the flowers weren't the same."

Heidi was listening with rapt attention.

"Then you made the colors I see here on the paper? Why, that's marvelous, Chel! How did you do it?"

"First I had an idea of squeezing flowers," he said. "Nothing came out of the petals. They were only spoiled and broken. So then I tried pressing blueberries and that gave me a beautiful purple to paint with. Then I found little red berries in the forest which made a deep, lovely color, and I found a flower at last from which I could make a yellow juice, and leaves from which I made green. But I had a hard time making brushes. I used my finger and stems of flowers, but it wasn't so good because the color wouldn't hold."

"Chel," interrupted Peter, seeing that he was absorbed by the question of painting, "hadn't you better tell us why you did not go to the villagers' houses for your meals as you were supposed to after your father died?"

"I went to several houses," said the boy, "but everywhere they scolded me. Then, when I was picking flowers in the meadow I sometimes met a goat and she gave me milk. The one I liked best was Distelfinck. She knew me so well she would run to meet me as soon as she saw me. She followed me everywhere. One day I said to her, 'Distelfinck, I will find you the best grasses that grow on the mountain, as much as I can pick, and in exchange you will give me milk.' "

"But that was not right, Chel," Peter said. "Since the goat belongs to the warden, her milk belongs to him, too. You can't make a bargain like that with someone else's goat!"

Chel was surprised at this.

"But I gave her so many nice things to eat," he protested. "None of the other goats were as well fed. One day I came near here, breaking my way through the underbrush. I was looking for a hiding place for my papers and colors—someplace where no one could find them and take them away. I came out of the woods there where the beautiful flowers grow, and as I ran from one to another, Distelfinck came jumping along at my side. She had followed me right through the forest and among all that underbrush. She is so clever! I told her to wait while I looked at the flowers; then we would go and pick some of the little plants that grow up here and that she likes so well. I had finished looking at the flowers and had a nice bunch for her. But she had disappeared. I called and called and then I heard her answer with little bleats the way she always does when I call her. But I couldn't see her anywhere. I looked down on the rocks but she wasn't there. At last I discovered that the bleating came from under that big ledge of rock. I climbed down on my hands and knees and found the entrance to this cave. Distelfinck bleated as much as to say, 'See, I found a beautiful room for you. You can hide your things here and nobody will ever find them.' That was what I wanted. I was perfectly safe and peaceful and I could work by myself. I built this table and bench. Distelfinck came again and again to see me. Once, instead of going around, she tried to come down straight above the cave. She slipped and fell and that was the time she broke her leg. You see, I didn't stone her. The warden lied! But I did stone him."

"That was very wrong," said Heidi. "You must never

stone anybody again, Chel. Promise me that you never will."

"Will you put me in the dungeon if I do?"

"I don't put children in the dungeon," Heidi said.

"But the dungeon is still there," Chel protested. "I know. I saw it when I came with the flowers—"

"Ah, Chel!" cried Heidi. "You've given yourself away. Now I know who brought me those beautiful flowers. They make me happy every day. And now that I know it was you who gave them to me, they will make me doubly happy. You thought of me then, even though you never came back. Why didn't you come back? Was it only because you were afraid of the dungeon?"

"I will never go to a school with a dungeon in it," he announced. "Never! Never as long as I live!"

"You must have been in the dungeon quite a few times," said Peter. "What was it like and why did the schoolmaster put you there?"

"He put me there every time he caught me drawing pictures," Chel said. "But there is a woman in the village who likes my pictures. It's the pastor's wife and she has been very kind to me. Several times she gave me bread in exchange for the pictures. Sometimes she gave me her boy's old clothes. She gave me the pot for those violets, too. But I made her promise first that she would never tell anybody I knew how to draw because then the schoolmaster would beat me or put me in the dungeon. She asked to have the schoolmaster leave so I guess that's why you're here," he added, turning to Heidi.

"I guess it is," Heidi agreed. "The pastor's wife used to be a schoolmistress herself, and she is a very good woman."

"But I don't go there anymore," Chel went on. "Once I was taking some pictures to her and some boys saw me and ran after me. They saw I was hiding something and they tried to take away my drawings. They said I stole them out of the shop. So I caught one of them and hit him so hard with my fist that he rolled down the hill on the rocks and made a hole in his head. That was the time you came out and called and I broke your flowerpot. Then when the warden said I threw stones at Distelfinck and they were going to put me in the dungeon again, you came and saved me! You helped me, so I thought I would give you the flowerpot the pastor's wife had given me—"

"And you were going to come to school, weren't you, until you saw the dungeon was still there?"

"Yes," Chel admitted. "But now you can't make me go."

"Poor Chel!" said Heidi, putting her hand affectionately on his shoulder. "I shall not try to make you go to school. But this savage life in the woods and these secret errands of yours are at an end now. You are coming home with me. My grandfather is old and I am

163

away at school all day and he is very lonely. He will like to have you with him to keep him company."

"Don't you think it would be better," Peter asked, "if he came to the village with me? The doctor took a great fancy to him and when he hears about his talent for drawing I'm sure he will want to educate him as he did you. You see, Heidi, it's best that he come with me."

"But grandfather is so lonely—"

"The doctor is so fond of him—"

Chel was looking from one face to the other, wondering if he might not soon wake up and find all this was only a dream. Before, no one had wanted him. He had been an outcast, stoned, imprisoned, hunted, living a savage existence and fearing everybody. Now two homes were open to him. Such good fortune seemed almost unbelievable.

"But if I go to live with the doctor, can I come back to my cave sometimes?" he finally asked.

"We'll come here again, together, many times," Heidi told him. "I'll show you how to use the paints I have at school and you can make copies of all the flowers that grow in the beautiful meadow just above your cave. But now let's go. Will you show us the way home again?"

"Shall I take all my things?" asked Chel, eyeing his treasured dabs of color and homemade brushes.

"Take your paintings and show them to the doctor,

but leave the rest. Then they will be here in your fortress when you return."

He gathered up his papers and went ahead to show them the way along the narrow ledge of rock leading up to the meadow. At the top, Peter and Heidi stopped and stood for a moment together looking at the chain of white peaks, the glittering pyramids of snow, and the garden that lay beyond them.

"We had to come up here," Heidi said at last. "Peter, you were right to bring me. Now I know why the grandfather must live on his mountain. And thank you, thank you a thousand times for the most wonderful surprise I ever had in my life."

17

CHEL SPENT the next night in the room at the doctor's where he had first tried to copy the white flowers. But this time when the doctor came in, he didn't try to hide what he was doing. He was busy copying the same painting on the back of an old piece of wrapping paper. The doctor gave him a fresh white sheet and two well-sharpened pencils. Then, taking the painting from the wall, he placed it conveniently in front of him on the table.

"There, now you can work all day long. You needn't go to school just yet. But before you make a smudge on the clean paper come along to the fountain with Brigitte and she will show you how to wash yourself."

Chel stared silently at his new working tools, remembered and said, "Thank you," and then ran off obediently to the fountain.

After school, Heidi stopped in to see how everything was going. But she stayed only a moment. She wanted to see the warden as soon as possible. He was just coming from the stable when she reached his house.

"How is Distelfinck doing?" she asked at once.

"For several days now she has seemed as spry as ever, even with her leg in splints," he replied. "Ah! She is a clever beast—intelligent! Different from the others! I wouldn't have parted with her. But there is one thing I notice since she broke her leg and I cannot understand it. She gives much more milk than before, but it is not the same. It lacks the fine, delicate flavor!"

Heidi did not think it was quite the moment to solve this puzzle for the warden although it was perfectly clear to her. She had other things to speak to him about.

"The doctor has taken Chel to live with him and may want to adopt him," she began. "And I have come to ask you to make a change in the schoolhouse so that he won't be afraid to return to school. It will be very simple. I only want the boards taken off that window in the cloakroom and glass put there in its place."

The warden stopped stock-still and looked at Heidi as though she were speaking a foreign language. It was several minutes before he found his voice. But when he did he surprised Heidi with the vehemence he put into his answer.

"I have said since the very beginning of school that

it wouldn't work having a woman for a teacher! But I, even I, didn't think it would come to this! Do you think I went to the trouble of fixing a dark room in the school only to tear it out again? And all for what? That the worst boy, a tramp known for miles around, won't be afraid to go to school. A good-for-nothing who hasn't anything better to do than abuse animals! *We are to make* over the school for *him?* Ah, yes! Ah, yes!"

He was so excited that his hands were shaking as he talked. Such hatred, such prejudice seemed almost unbelievable to Heidi when kindness was all the boy needed.

"About Chel, I will say nothing," she retorted. "You have such decided notions that I could never change them with words. Chel will show you what he is and that will have more effect. As for my request, there is nothing extraordinary about it. The dungeon is there, and there is not a mother in Dörfli who would not like to see it made into a cloakroom again. If you refuse to do it, then you can look for someone else to teach your school. I refuse to be responsible for frightening little children—"

Immediately little Nanni, who had not lost one word of the conversation between the teacher and her father, ran as fast as she could to the house next door.

"Germaine! Germaine! Hurry up! Come quickly!" she cried to her friend who was busy helping her mother in the kitchen.

Germaine came running out, drying her hands.

"The teacher is going to leave! What shall we do?" panted Nanni in her excitement.

"What's that! Don't we do everything she says? And don't we just love the sewing class and the art class? What does she want to leave for?" asked Germaine.

"Because my father boarded up the window to the cloakroom!" cried Nanni and ran on to the next house.

Germaine, too, ran off with news of the terrible tragedy. By evening the whole village knew that Heidi wished to leave, but no one knew why. "Because the warden boarded up the window!" was all they could make out.

When the day's work was done everyone, being more or less affected by the news, came out and took the road to the warden's house. When he saw all the people coming up the hill he came out, too, thinking that Chel was up to some new prank and that the village was up in arms again. But what he heard was very different. The women attacked him angrily and demanded to know why he was sending Heidi away. If Heidi wanted anything extraordinary she most probably had her reasons for it. They, the mothers, felt they knew better than anyone else her value in the town and they would never consent to allowing such a good teacher to leave!

In turn, the men arrived, one after another, to see what was happening. They felt the same. Why allow anyone so good and so devoted to leave? Since Heidi

had been teaching the school everything seemed to have changed for the better. The school was hardly recognizable, so neat and clean had it been kept. The children were clean and orderly and rarely quarreled. No, they would certainly not agree to let the teacher leave. What was this window that had been boarded up anyway?

When at last the warden was allowed to speak, he explained that the thing in itself wasn't difficult. It was a simple question of putting in a window and making a cloakroom out of the schoolhouse cell. But what was absolutely out of the question was the stand the teacher had taken for that rogue Chel, whom she had persuaded the doctor to adopt and take to live with him.

On all sides were exclamations of surprise. The villagers thought Heidi must have made some unreasonable demand. This was not only reasonable but right and just. And, as for Chel, the fact that Heidi had taken him in hand proved that she was no weakling.

Then and there everyone offered to help with the alterations on the school. The warden was completely taken aback.

"She is all right, I must admit—but that good-for-nothing, bah! You'll see! You'll see!" he grumbled, going back into his house.

Several weeks later when the children came to class as usual, they saw a well-dressed boy sitting before a little table by the window drawing. He was copying a picture in beautiful colors and his head was bent low over his work.

"He must be an artist to be able to copy that picture!" whispered one of the girls as she slipped into her place.

The boy was so intent upon his work that he didn't turn his head to right or left and the class could not see his face. But suddenly sharp-eyed Germaine leaned toward her neighbor's ear and whispered:

"It's Chel! Look! I'll bet you anything it's Chel!"

"It is not Chel," retorted Nanni. "My father said just today that we'd see what good-for-nothingness he's been up to all this time he hasn't come to school!"

"It *is* Chel," declared Germaine obstinately.

After class, she stopped on her way out and looked around from the back, just as the boy lifted his head. He wore shining new shoes, a white shirt, and a suit that was as clean and new as any of the Sunday best in the village—it was Chel! She recognized him at once. But his whole expression was changed. Germaine took one more good look and then ran out to announce the miracle to all her friends waiting in the school yard.

No one lingered on the road that day. All the children in the school ran home as fast as they could with the news.

For four weeks Chel, burning with enthusiasm, had worked without interruption under Doctor Reboux's excellent direction. He made such progress that even

Heidi and Peter, who had great confidence in him, were surprised. But during all this time the doctor had kept him apart from the other children, first, to observe him and know him well before he took his place in the schoolroom and, in the second place, because he wanted nothing of the old Chel to appear, but a new Chel completely transformed.

During this time Heidi had often gone back to Chel's cave where, with her splendid bright colors, she helped him copy the lovely flowers that grew in what she and Peter had decided to call "the enchanted garden." As they worked there together Chel's eyes glowed with happiness because he could draw and paint now as much as he liked without having to hide away from everybody and without the problem of manufacturing his own brushes and colors. When Heidi praised his work and told him that if he continued like that he would surely be a great artist, Chel's heart was filled with joy. Only once in a while a shadow veiled his sparkling eyes and an expression of fear passed over his face as of old. But when Heidi questioned him, he managed to brighten up and tell her it was nothing.

After studying a painting of some wild flowers which Chel had made, Heidi remarked, "Your work delights me, but why did you make these anemones a different pink from those in the picture you are copying?"

"I know those flowers so well," said Chel quickly. "They are just the color I made them. It is exactly that same color and not the color in this picture. I've often looked at them growing near this cave. There are lots of them here."

Heidi smiled. "Then you were right to paint them this way. You see, it will help your work a lot, knowing the flowers the way you do. I must remember to tell this to the doctor."

Chel's face fairly shone with joy, but the moment Heidi mentioned the doctor it became overshadowed and this time it seemed to stay that way.

"What's the matter?" demanded Heidi. "You certainly don't mind if I tell the doctor about your painting?"

"No. Oh, no! That isn't it," burst out Chel, turning his face away.

"But what? Tell me once and for all what is troubling you, Chel," urged Heidi.

"Each time I feel terribly happy, so happy that I could cry out for joy, I see a picture before my eyes. I see the doctor leaving me again or telling me again that I am free. Then there I am, all alone, forced to throw stones to protect myself and hiding off somewhere to be able to paint. Then one day the warden will catch me again and beat me and there won't be anybody to help me because I don't belong to anybody—not anybody! Then everything will be finished! All over!" said the boy despairingly.

"Chel!" exclaimed Heidi, taking his hand. "You

must never think that again. You belong to the doctor. He took you to keep always and he wants to be a father to you. You know that a child belongs to his father?"

"Yes," said Chel doubtfully, "but are you sure?"

"Come home now," she replied, "and the doctor will tell you himself. Then you'll be sure! You will never have to worry about it again in all your life."

When they reached home and the doctor assured Chel that everything Heidi had told him was true, he took the kind hand that was held out to him and squeezed it as though he would never let it go. He wiped his eyes and smiled up at the doctor.

"Now when someone wants to hurt me, can I say, too, 'I'll tell my father!'? And you won't ever leave me?" he asked.

The doctor put his arm around him affectionately and told him once more that from now on he was his little son and would have a home with him as long as he lived.

Chel Pays a Debt

18

THE TRANSFORMATION of Chel gave the villagers something to talk about for a long while to come. Furthermore, they gave Heidi credit for everything good and desirable that happened for miles around. There was not a person in Dörfli who didn't feel that the worst thing that could happen to the community would be for Heidi to leave. Even the warden was convinced of it.

Until the end of the following autumn everything continued to go on as well as it had begun. Chel worked on silently in the classroom with the other children. In that way it was simpler for Heidi to supervise his ·painting. But he remained apart and became very reserved. In the classroom he showed himself to be as hard a worker in his studies as he was in painting and he soon surpassed many of the boys who used to taunt him.

For Chel, the happiest moment of the day was in the evening. Then the doctor sat close to him and while he painted and drew, he read stories to him. Usually they were stories of poor boys, like himself, who had become great and famous. He told him of schools in Lausanne and in Paris where professors held classes in drawing and painting.

On Sundays Chel put his books and lessons aside and often, after church, he and the doctor went together to the meadow up on the mountain, where hardy flowers still bloomed. Heidi and Peter were the only ones in the village who knew where they went.

As they passed, the villagers remarked, "It's beyond me to understand how such a little tramp could change into the neatest and nicest boy in the village!"

Only one other living creature knew of this lovely garden, high up on the mountain, and she came often, limping slightly, to stand affectionately close to Chel. It was Distelfinck. Chel had not forgotten where to find the delicious grasses and plants she enjoyed so well. He loved this old goat as a dear friend. But when Heidi and Peter came along to the garden, she divided her affection between them.

Toward the end of the winter the doctor sent the following letter to a professor he knew in Frankfurt:

Dear Professor:

Some time ago you asked me if I knew of anyone who was familiar with the rare flowers which
bloom in the Alps and who was a fine enough
artist to make the illustrations for your textbooks
on botany. If you are still looking for someone to
do this work, I can recommend my adopted son,
Chel, who has all the qualifications. He not only
has a profound knowledge of flowers but a real
artistic talent as well.

I shall look forward with pleasure to hearing
from you. In the meantime, I remain

Yours sincerely,

Doctor Reboux

Only a few days later, the reply came. So, in the
early spring, as soon as the first flowers appeared, the
doctor sent Chel to select the most perfect specimens
of each variety. These he placed in a glass and told
him to draw them as well as he possibly could.

Sometimes Heidi and Peter accompanied Chel when
he went up to the meadow to choose the flowers he was
going to draw. Chel could not decide which were the
happiest moments for him—those when he was at work
with the doctor leaning over him directing and helping, or those high up in the meadow, which was no
longer a refuge but a beautiful garden that he knew
and loved so well. He often felt like throwing himself

on the ground and gathering all the flowers into his arms.

To Heidi these trips up the mountain were a needed change from the routine of the classroom. Often she returned feeling rested and refreshed and closer to her childhood than she had been since the days when she used to go to the pasture with Peter.

It pleased Peter that Distelfinck so often followed them. The little goat soon found out that Chel went to the mountain every day, so she never failed to come and receive her favorite herbs and grasses from his hand and linger close to his side until it was time to leave. Peter explained all this to Thoni so when they came into view of the village Chel would say good-bye to the goat.

"Go back to the goatherd, Distelfinck," he would tell her. "It is better if you are seen returning with the flock."

One evening when Chel came in from a trip to the meadow the doctor handed him a package.

"Chel, you no longer need me to help you on your way," he said. "All this belongs to you. It is in payment for your beautiful work." And he showed him the bank notes the envelope had contained.

At the sight of the money Chel was too surprised to speak. Then, with an unhappy look, he turned away from the table.

"Why, Chel! Aren't you glad to receive this money?

It's the first salary you've earned!" exclaimed the doctor.

"You don't want me to stay with you anymore now that I've earned it," said Chel. "In that case, I don't want the money."

"You didn't understand," the doctor replied. "I only meant that no one in the village thought you were capable of working and earning a living. Now they will see what you can do! The professor who sends you this money is so pleased with your work that he wants you to continue copying flowers for his books. After this first book there will be others for which you will make the illustrations, and each new volume will pay you as this one has. You will see, Chel! The more perfect you become, the more work you will have to do. That is what makes me so happy!"

"This belongs to you and the teacher," said Chel, pointing to the money. "You taught me everything I know."

"No. It was your work. Neither of us would want your money. Put it aside for the moment unless you want something. Is there anything you would like to do with it?"

"Yes. There is something," said Chel.

"How much will you need?"

He thought for a moment and then announced, "I will need six of those bank notes."

The doctor was surprised and looked at the boy, but

he had confidence in him and decided to allow him to spend his money as he pleased. Chel took it and went out. Not far off he came to a small house on the edge of the village. He went directly into the main room which was empty, put one bank note down on the table, and cried to the woman in the kitchen, "Paid!"

Running from one to the other, he entered six houses in each of which he had taken his meals and slept overnight. In each one he said the same thing. But when he went into the sixth house and put his bank note down, he cried, "Paid to the community!"

For he had never forgotten the day they told him that he was an expense to the village—good-for-nothing that he was, who couldn't appreciate a good bed!

19

ALL DÖRFLI was in an uproar when they learned that Chel not only earned money, but that his first thought had been to pay back what no one else would even have considered a debt. Chel, the good-for-nothing, had at last won the respect of the village. It was true that a very little time before he had been a tramp, and it was Heidi who had brought about this miracle. At no price would they ever consider allowing her to leave the school.

"You see what you've done," Peter scolded her one evening, as they trudged together up the footpath that led to the grandfather's house on the Alm. "You've made yourself so indispensable to the village that you won't be allowed to give up teaching and when the uncle gets too feeble to do things for himself, how is he going to manage alone up there on the mountain?"

"I've thought of that myself," said Heidi with a sigh. "I try my best to make everybody happy and this is my reward."

"Well, teaching was what you wanted."

"Was it? I'm not so sure about it now, Peter," Heidi confessed. "Sometimes in the schoolroom I feel shut in, the way you said you did in the doctor's house. Then I long to be up on the mountain all day long where I can look out and see the whole valley and stretch my arms and feel free. Besides, the grandfather needs me. So often he says he is growing old and calls me to pray with him. Yesterday he said perhaps this would be his last winter—and he had such a look in his eyes when he said it. It frightened me, Peter! It was as though he were seeing something beyond—something that the grandmother saw when she began to long for her garden. I can't bear it if he dies!" she cried out in sudden anguish. "I shall be all alone. No, Peter. I shall not teach again in the fall. No matter what the warden says, I cannot go back."

"Then who will take your place, Heidi?"

"I'll write to Jamy," she decided. "Jamy loved it here. She wanted to come again for the vacation and I shall write and ask her to come and stay and teach the school."

Jamy was delighted with the invitation. But when she arrived a cloud hung over the house on the Alm. The grandfather was very ill. He said it was only old age, but he seemed to be in a great deal of pain and kept calling for Heidi.

"I am here, Grandfather," she kept telling him. Then, when he saw it was true, he would call out for Peter.

Jamy came in and went over by the bed and took his hand. Her voice was warm and comforting.

"I am here now," she said, "and Heidi will not need to leave you. I am here to teach the children so you will not be left alone."

"That is not it," he replied. "When I am gone, Heidi will be left alone. Who will keep my house? Who will take care of Schwanli and Barli? Tell Heidi I want her. Heidi! Heidi!"

"I'm here, Grandfather," she replied. "I'm right here beside your bed. Jamy and I are both here. I won't go away."

He fell back on his pillows, sighed, and took Heidi's hand.

"Read me some hymns," he said. "Those you used to read to the blind grandmother. Send Jamy after them. Peter must have them."

The hymns were brought, and Peter came with them. He sat beside the bed quietly listening as Heidi read in her clear, sweet voice:

"Crosses and sorrow
    May end with the morrow,
    Stormiest seas
    Shall sink into peace;
The wild winds are hushed and the sunshine re-
    turns."

Heidi paused a moment and it seemed as if the wind
in the pine trees outside paused with her, hushed as the
hymn said, listening. On the grandfather's face was a
look of peace and satisfaction.

"Is the pain better, Grandfather?" she asked.

"Yes, yes," he said. "There is no pain. Go on, Heidi.
There is more to the hymn."

Tears stood in Heidi's eyes as she read:

"So fullness of rest,
    And the calm of the blest,
    Are waiting me there
    In that garden most fair,
That home for which daily my spirit here yearns."

There was silence in the room when the hymn was
finished. Only the sighing of the pine trees outside
and the grandfather's breathing could be heard.

Is it true, Heidi wondered, that when people are old
they begin to have a longing for high places? Did the
grandfather long for the garden beyond her sight, just
as she and Peter longed for the mountains when every-

thing seemed to close about them down in the village?

"Now play it," the grandfather was saying in a low voice. "I want to hear you play the hymn on your violin."

Heidi took up her bow and the music trembled and sobbed. There was longing in it—Heidi's longing for life so great that it almost choked her when she looked out over the white mountain peaks and saw them glow suddenly in the fire of the sunset. The grandfather's longing was in it, too, and Peter's restlessness.

Suddenly Peter stood up.

"I'm going outside for a while," he said. "I must think something through."

Heidi saw that he wanted to be alone and only nodded, laying aside her violin. The grandfather's eyes were closed and he was sleeping without pain.

"The music soothes him," Jamy said. "When he wakes up perhaps we can coax him to take some milk."

It was midnight when he awoke.

"Where's Peter?" he asked, his eyes fixed on Heidi.

"He went outside to think," Heidi replied. "He seemed to have something on his mind, Grandfather. Are you feeling any better?"

"So he had something on his mind, did he? Yes, yes," said the old man. "I'm feeling much better. It's about time that boy had something on his mind."

The following morning when Peter, quite unexpectedly, asked Heidi to marry him, she exclaimed in the utmost surprise, "Why, Peter! I think *that* must have been what I wanted. That was the reason I wanted to stay in Dörfli."

They planned a street wedding so that everyone in the village could take part in the beautiful ceremony. When they told the grandfather about it, his old eyes sparkled.

"You must get well for the wedding," Heidi urged him anxiously. "You have nothing to fret about now and you're sure to get well. Peter will always look after me, just as you have. And we'll both look after you and give you the best of care. We'll look after the goats, too, and we'll live here in this house where we can always look up to the mountains. Grandfather, we're going to be so happy, you and Peter and I. You will get well for the wedding, won't you? Please!"

"Yes," he said. "I'll get well. I'll wear my green Sunday suit and march along with the best of them. Miss my little girl's wedding? Well, I should think not. Of course your old grandfather will get well, Heidi—for the wedding."

True to his promise, the grandfather was up in a week. He cut the grass and hauled in the wood and worked about the house with all of his old vigor. Heidi was delighted. There was nothing to mar the beauty of her wedding day.

Clara came to the wedding—a Clara Heidi hardly would have known for the stately lady she had become.

Jamy sent for the little sister she always used to speak of when she and Heidi were in school together. The sister was to join the wedding procession, carrying the wheat.

Dörfli was noted for its quaint customs. This day men and women were garbed in their holiday best. Bright shawls were to be seen everywhere. They were embroidered in every shade of pink, gold, yellow, and blue. Brigitte wore a deep purple shawl over a stiffly starched blouse with wide, puffed sleeves. The doctor came along beside her in his shiny black suit with a stiff collar standing about his ears. Chel's hat was tall and red and he wore an eagle's feather.

Music heralded the wedding party. The musicians played on flutes, pipes, and old-time stringed lutes. An accordion player in a red waistcoat headed the band and the others followed.

Next came the bride, her cheeks glowing with happiness. Heidi was wearing a bridal gown of purest silk. Her wreath was a creation of flowers from her own enchanted garden wound about with white ribbon. Peter walked beside her, tall and proud. The grandfather was not far behind, marching along as jauntily as the others, resplendent in his green suit. Then came all the schoolchildren of Dörfli with Jamy to keep them in order, leading them in a beautiful old folk song.

How picturesque it all was! How gay the music sounded! The solemn rites in the church had not taken away one bit of the gaiety or the laughter. It was a day never to be forgotten. How glad Heidi was that she had been faithful to her own people, that she had come back to Dörfli where she belonged—back to Dörfli and to Peter. Suddenly she remembered a quaint custom of the villagers and bent to take off her shoe.

Everywhere children were throwing flowers. Now Heidi seized her wedding slipper and, aiming it carefully, threw it into the crowd. It landed at Chel's feet and all about him were heard cries of, "Good luck, Chel! Good luck with your painting!"

"Thank you, Heidi," he called out, "for throwing me the lucky slipper!"

The wedding procession passed on down the street to the village square where tables were arranged for the wedding feast. So the music played on and there was dancing and singing far into the night. But Heidi and Peter slipped away early. On their wedding day, of all days, they must not miss seeing the sun set fire to the snow on the mountain. As they watched, the grandfather watched with them and when the splendor had faded, he said, "You see, Heidi, it fades only to return again tomorrow."

"It is a promise," said Peter. "But however many times it may return it will never see a happier day than this."